SADDLE BOW SLIM

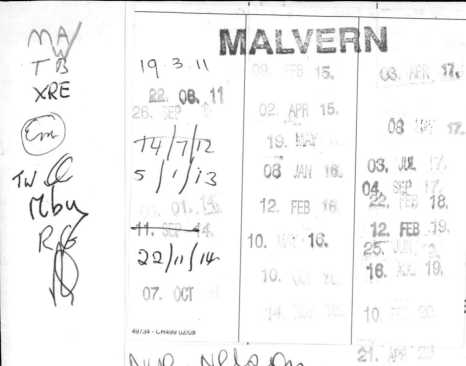

SADDLE BOW SLIM

Nelson C. Nye

WHEELER

CHIVERS

This Large Print edition is published by Wheeler Publishing, Waterville, Maine USA and by BBC Audiobooks Ltd, Bath, England.

Published in 2006 in the U.S. by arrangement with Golden West Literary Agency.

Published in 2006 in the U.K. by arrangement with Golden West Literary Agency.

U.S. Softcover   1-59722-227-5   (Western)
U.K. Hardcover 10: 1 4056 3747 1   (Chivers Large Print)
U.K. Hardcover 13: 978 1 405 63747 3
U.K. Softcover 10: 1 4056 3748 X   (Camden Large Print)
U.K. Softcover 13: 978 1 405 63748 0

The text of this Large Print edition is unabridged.
Other aspects of the book may vary from the original edition.

Set in 16 pt. Plantin by Christina S. Huff.

Printed in the United States on permanent paper.

British Library Cataloguing-in-Publication Data available

Library of Congress Cataloging-in-Publication Data

Nye, Nelson C. (Nelson Coral), 1907–
    Saddle Bow Slim / By Nelson C. Nye.
      p. cm.
    ISBN 1-59722-227-5 (lg. print : sc : alk. paper)
    1. Large type books.   I. Title.
PS3527.Y33S2 2006
  813´.54—dc22   2006001356

SADDLE BOW SLIM

1

DAVID AND GOLIATH

When Helvetia's peace marshal turned in his star a good many hard-cased citizens drew the first easy breath they had taken in some time and there weren't any tears shed about it. Whit Brand had sure carved a name for himself and it wasn't the kind to get remembered with pleasure. If he never came back that would be soon enough, and young Whit had the same notion.

He was plumb fed up with that thankless town, and when he saddled his big bay gelding and took off east through the mountains, he was sure enough glad to forget it. He was heading for a land that was far away, the boom silver camp of Galeyville, to discover what color a girl's eyes were and if those were freckles he had seen in her picture.

Some guys, perhaps, wouldn't have cared a whole lot, but that was the kind of a jigger Brand was — unexpected. He

7

hadn't the look of a town tamer, being young for that and kind of open in the face. You could tell he was a riding man by looking at his legs, but that was far as looks would take you. In a country where most gents inclined toward whiskers, Brand didn't sport so much as a mustache. This had given him a dewy, kind of unweaned appearance which subsequent developments had proved quite unwarranted.

He had looked like a dude just stepped off the train. With his guileless eyes and friendly grin, he'd been judged plumb gentle by those who bothered to carve notches in their gun butts. It was a shock to discover he could be so deceptive.

Helvetia's storekeepers had been loudly wailing their need of a marshal. When Brand came riding in one day the town sports thought it would be quite a joke to saddle him with this thankless job. Free drinks flowed like a flood that day and they got the tin pinned on him. It wasn't till a couple of days afterwards that they began to suspicion what fools they had been. They blamed it all on the merchants, these having contended a marshal would prove good insurance against the bully-puss manners of roving gunslicks. None suggested Brand had not proved so. He was a red-striped whizzer from who laid the chunk, but there was such a thing as carrying it too far. "I was hired," Brand said, "to clean up this town." "Sure," said the sports, "to clean it up but not to bury it!"

Brand packed one gun, like most guys, politely stashed in a holster. But he kept a second one handy in the waistband of his pants and the handle of a hide-out third peeped demurely from his armpit and how were you supposed to know which one of them he would reach for?

Deceitful as a woman's watch. Strong as a Brahman bull, that kid, and race-horse swift in the clinches. A forty-five caliber article got up to look like a cap pistol. Mad was a mighty mild way to describe them when the town sports belatedly discovered their error.

But if they were glad to see the last of him, Brand was equally pleased to be shed of them and all the thankless tasks which their orneriness had made for him. That gentle grin which had so enraged them crossed his mouth again as he sat with a knee casually curled round the horn of his saddle and considered the face he had shaken from the wallet with IRA McLOWN stamped in gold letters on it — on the wallet, that is.

9

It was the kind of a face a guy dreamed about when he sat staring into a campfire. Only he sure wished he knew if those were freckles. He could sure sit the bag for a redhead with freckles, freckled gals and flea-bitten nags being potent medicine to his way of thinking. He put the picture away with a sigh and dreamily stared off into the distance.

With so little to go on, only the look of a face, a man had to take an awful lot on trust, but Whit was willing. He could see she had plenty of heart girth and he knew her front name was Taisy — she had written it, with love, on the back of her picture.

"Taisy," Whit said, with the look of a dying calf on his face. He sighed again, gathered up his reins and, with another heaved sigh, kneed his horse toward the faraway blue that was shrouding the slopes of the Cherrycow Mountains.

He wasn't the kind to admit he had pitched up a hundred-a-month job on account of nothing more than a strange girl's picture. He said he'd quit that job because he plain hadn't liked it. There wasn't any future to that kind of job but a quick-shoveled grave on the side of some hill or at the bottom of a gulch where the storm

10

waters howled. Let your Bat Mastersons have it. Whit Brand didn't crave any part of it.

Maybe, like they said, he was a heap too fiddle-footed ever to amount to anything in the world. Maybe they were right when they called him Saddle Bow Slim with all the contempt they'd have given the word "drifter." Perhaps he was just a saddle bum; but one thing was sure — he wasn't hunting for glory. He wasn't looking for anything but a redhead with freckles and, if the chance came his way, a gray horse with the same. That wasn't asking too much of luck, was it?

Whit felt a heap better than he had for long months as he climbed up into those wild, rugged mountains and drew in great gulps of invigorating air.

Mountains was the place for young folks. A man could chop him out a cabin for nothing and grub was to hand; all you had to do was shoot it and drop it in the pot. Why any gent would choose to live in a town when country like this was to be had for the taking was more than young Whit could savvy.

He was as happy as he'd ever been in his life as he went pirooting up that Galeyville trail with the windswept blue of the sky overhead and the cowbirds singing in the brush all about him. Once he saw a big buck mule-deer skitter up out of a creek bed and go busting off through the chaparral. Time and again quail startled his horse and the smell of the pines was God's own nectar; and the days lazed along right pleasantly.

There was a chance, to be sure, he might have figured this wrong. That girl might not be at Galeyville. The wallet and those letters might not have any connection, but the letters, anyway, had been addressed to that place — they'd been written to a fellow called Stampede Smith. Whit reckoned someone up there ought to know her, else how come Smith was packing her picture?

He would find her, by grab, if he had to go clean to Texas!

It was almost sundown on the third day out when Whit got his first look at Galeyville. He was high in the crags of the Cherrycows then, and seen from there, as he looked down through the pines, the town looked a lot more like some ant hill than like the owlhoot capital of all Arizona. He could not make out so much as one building; all he could see was a gray plume of smoke and the raw earthy splotches that were mine dumps.

But he laughed in the sunlight and shadows of the pines. No matter what it looked like, that town sprawled there in all its iniquity was Curly Bill's stronghold; it could give roaring Charlston every card in the deck and outshoot Tombstone with both eyes shut. It was a wilder place than Tascosa ever had been. Hardly five minutes slipped past, day or night, without the accompanying roar of six-shooters. It was the noisiest town this side of Hell.

This was Curly Bill's country and he was its boss. From that little old mesa down in Turkey Creek Canyon, he ruled this region like a feudal baron. He was a big six-footer and built like a blacksmith, a blue-shirted white-hatted Texican who never said a word about his buried past and covered the present with a bold free laugh and the deadly repute of his way with a pistol. He could ride day or night with forty men at his back. He lived like a king off the fat of the land and the tribute that lesser crooks dared not refuse him. He stole herds of cattle wherever he found them. Nothing was too big for Curly Bill to tackle, be it a caravan of smugglers up from Mexico City or just some grand lady fresh arrived from the East. He ran off Army-post horses and was described in Congress as a "menace!"

Whit Brand looked forward to meeting this rustler who could snatch the U.S. Cavalry horseless.

You wouldn't never have guessed Brand had never known his folks and had gotten his name from a tomato-can label the night he ran off from Arkansaw Tummer, but such was the case. Ark Tummer was out on one of his benders when the trail herd straggled past his place that day. Like he did most of the time, Ark had just started in to gather him up a talking load but, like he did most of the time also, he had forgot when to stop. When night's loamy blackness rolled across the land the kid went after the trail herd. The first thing the trail boss asked him was: "Did you cut yore stick from thet spread back yonder?"

The kid looked up at him kind of uneasily. "Well, yes," he said finally. "I'm allowin' you'd prob'ly of run away too if you got won in a card game by a feller like Tummer."

The trail boss rasped a hand through his whiskers. He studied the kid and rasped his whiskers again. "How come yore folks —"

"They're dead — they got skelped by Injuns, mister. An' I'm a sight too old t' git

14

manhandled reg'lar an' I'm reckonin' I've had enough of it."

"How old would thet be?" the trail boss said. "I don't notice no wrinkles around yore horns."

The kid pushed a sweaty lock back from his eyes and looked straight into the trail boss' face.

"I'm a-comin' fifteen! I been a long time weaned an' I'm a right smart hand around cattle, mister." The kid's expression got a little desperate then. "I ain't allowin' t' go back if'n you hire me or not."

The trail boss flattened out a grin and said, scowling: "What would a feller hev t' yell t' git hold of you?"

And that was when the kid saw the tomato can. It flashed like silver in the light of the fire on which some waddy had just heaved an armful of brush. *Whitman's Brand Giant Hand-Packed Tomatoes — Best In The West.* That was what the label said, but the kid cut her down to plain Whit Brand and gave it to the boss for a handle.

It was along about first-drink time in the morning when Brand followed Turkey Creek into its canyon and rode through a tangle of ash and sycamore to a place where the mountains fell back from a mesa that was patched up in green with live oak and juniper. There was a fine flight of buzzards wheeling over the place, and by these tokens, Whit reckoned he was getting pretty close to the jump-off. The trail, increasingly cluttered with bottles, lazily angled up the side of the mesa, and Brand, with two horses in tow which he hadn't had yesterday, put the creek's sound behind him and commenced thinking.

Cresting the rim, he pulled up for a moment and sat back in his saddle looking over the town. His face appeared a little incredulous, and there was vexed disgust in the curl of his lip.

So this was the place that had caused so much uproar! Whit studied the scene with a jaundiced eye. Why it wasn't any different from forty-eight other towns Whit had been into . . . the same dingy shacks with their dusty false fronts, cob-webbed windows and hitch rails of reins-polished poles. The same up-and-down sort of warped plank walks, the same board awnings, the selfsame dust. He had looked for Curly Bill's town to be different, but the only difference he could see was that the drab sand-scoured buildings of this miserable place had all been shoved up on one side of the street. In an uneven straggling line they stood like a rank of Mexican soldiers, apathetic, indifferent, in the shimmering heat that boiled off the hoof-tracked dust before them. All but one, that is, Nick Babcock's bar, a place notorious for the caliber of its booze, its roughhouse brawls and loose women.

There was a big live-oak growing in front of this place, and sprawled in its shade sat a guy in a rocker with a bottle of beer loosely gripped in one paw and a six-shooter jumping in the other every time a gopher popped up from its hole by the corner.

Brand judged this gent wasn't much of a shot because there weren't any dead ones lying around. There were cow horses hitched to some of the tie rails and a wagon was stopped by Shotwell's store; and off a bit, a couple or three doors beyond it, four-five gents were busily wagging their jaws beneath the wide awning of Jack Dall's saloon.

Brand rasped his own jaw. He stared at the rocker. The six-gun shooter was a big burly sport with the length of his face wrapped up in a bandage. This was Curly Bill Graham, the boss rustler himself, but Whit didn't know the boss rustler from grape juice.

"Excuse me, mister," Whit said, smiling freely, "but who takes care of dead road-agents here?"

2

IN THE PALM
OF GOD'S HAND

Curly Bill wasn't the kind of a guy you could hurry.

He was a big-boned feller with plenty of meat and looked like he could twist bar iron with his fingers. His dark swarthy face appeared considerably surprised to be hearing himself addressed in that manner. His black eyes narrowed up at Brand and he looked him over quite a spell without speaking.

"What was that you said?"

Brand hooked a thumb toward the led horses back of him. "Who takes care of dead road-agents here?"

Curly Bill never took his eyes from Brand's face. He looked like he just plain couldn't believe it. And he couldn't. It wasn't reasonable to think any feller could be so plumb foolish as to come at him with a question like that.

He shoved back his hat with the neck of the bottle and stared at the kid in considerable silence. Like he couldn't seem to get his mind made up, he slanched a look over Whit Brand's outfit, and his wide upper lip twisted down disparagingly as his glance passed over the nearer led horse. It was the kind of a nag no high-riding man would care to have in his company, a flea-bitten gray with collar marks.

But when Bill's glance touched the other one, the second led horse, it looked like he was going to choke to death.

With an outraged oath he came out of his chair.

He stomped to the horse, beer and gun still in hand, like his eyes couldn't believe what they saw in the saddle.

It was a man, belly down, and he was very dead.

"Know him?" Brand said.

"Do I know him!" Bill roared. "Why, you straggly-haired —"

But Graham might as well have saved his breath. Whit Brand wasn't even listening. He had turned clear around in his saddle and was intently staring toward Shotwell's store. A young thing had just come out of it with her lithe tanned arms filled with bundles. She had a sorrel mane piled high on her head and her high-heeled boots tapped gay little sounds from the spur-raked planks of the whoppy-jawed walk as she wended her way past the saloon fronts.

Whit Brand stared after her, scarcely breathing.

It was her, all right. No mistake about it. The girl of the picture — redheaded and freckled!

The gents on the porch of Jack Dall's saloon had left off their talk and were likewise watching. And a feller dashed out of a nearby alley and ducked up the steps of a doorway marked MARSHAL and pretty near yanked the door off its hinges he was in such a lather to get inside. And another guy came right out of that place and gaited his steps down the walk behind her. And none of these things Brand noticed at all, so filled was his mind with her radiant loveliness.

The girl continued on past Mc-Conaghey's bar, and Larry Garcia, coming out of a building, said something to her and she smiled at him and paused to stand a while chatting. The gent that was trailing her paused also, leaning his weight against Phil McCarthy's until she got under way again, after which he too got himself into motion.

Brand hardly noticed this stir and bustle. In the flesh Miss Taisy was beyond all believing. "Bee trees," Whit breathed, "is plumb gall beside her," and on a sudden impulse, he kneed his big bay into movement. He was like a guy in a trance, cater-cornering over there through the drifted yellow dust; like the Wise Man following the star he moved, pulling the flea-bitten led horse after him, leaving the corpse-burdened one beside Bill. Curly Bill was just ruining his voice for nothing, because Whit Brand was stone deaf to anything but that girl. He was wondering what the rest of her name was and how he was going to scrape up an acquaintance. It was a cinch he couldn't fetch out that picture, and only a fool would have mentioned Smith. She wouldn't be knowing a feller like Smith. She might not know that McLown gent, neither, and the chances were McLown was dead, else how come Smith had been packing his wallet?

Suppose this McLown should be Taisy's father!

Now there was a thought, and no pleasant one neither. Telling that girl how he had found her dad's wallet in a dead gun shark's pocket was one way of meeting her that Brand didn't care for.

In the meantime the bay was fetching him closer, packing him toward the Lone Star Grub toward which Miss Taisy appeared to be headed.

No, Whit decided, he wouldn't speak just yet. Time enough for that after he'd cased the town and got a line on its politics. This wasn't a place to go off half cocked. This was Curly Bill's hangout, he reminded himself,. and a darned good place to sing low and sweet like.

Shepherd T. Towser, one of the voters Curly Bill had fetched back from the San Simon election, came wagging his tail behind Sandy King, one of Curly Bill's ruffians, who had stepped from McCarthy's and was watching the girl with bright-eyed approval while he took off his hat and finger-combed his bleached hair. King muttered to Garcia. Garcia ducked under the nearest hitch rail and went hiking down the road in the direction of Galey's smelter.

As Garcia passed Babcock's a whiskered gent ran out and called after him, but Garcia didn't stop. He ducked into the brush and kept on going. The whiskered man swore. He snatched out his pistol and let fly a few rounds with a face purely wicked. A second whiskered man limped

23

out of the brush where Garcia had vanished and picked up his bullet-creased hat in black silence. "Say — excuse me, mister," called the man with the pistol, "I shore didn't know you was in them bushes."

Whit Brand, still urging his horse toward the Lone Star, never noticed this by-play. Miss Taisy had just reached the hash house and had climbed the steps and had a hand stretched out to unlatch the screen door. Instead of doing so, however, she turned around, facing Whit but looking on past him. Her cheeks gone stiff and her glance gone stormy, she shortened her gaze and looked squarely at Whit.

"I think," she said scornfully, "your friend's calling you." And she whirled, white with anger, and went sloshing into the Lone Star, letting the screen door slam behind her.

Brand cuffed back his hat and looked after her, puzzled.

Friend, she had said. What friend? And why that tone?

He twisted his lean body around in the saddle. His startled eyes saw the man from the rocker, beer and gun still in hand, coming over the ground like an overgrown scorpion, tail up, and dust spurting. The big gent's face, inside the white bandage, looked black as the belly of a horse at midnight.

He was sure enough mad and wasn't throttling his feelings.

He came larruping up and gave Brand a look that would have knocked down an oak post. The way he was waving that gun was plumb reckless.

"By Gawd, are you *deef?*"

Whit frowned at him, puzzled. He said, "Not as I know of."

"Ain't you never seen no woman before?"

Brand seemed to put a heap of thought to that question. Then he suddenly grinned. "No, I ain't," he said, "not no sorrel-topped filly like that one! They keep her stabled round here? Does she pass this way frequent?"

Curly Bill aired another batch of cusswords. "I wanta know, by Gawd, what happened to Mell Snyder!"

Brand's attention seemed in danger of wandering again. He had twisted his face toward the Lone Star Grub and his inquiring eye was curiously fixed on the shad-bellied man who had just drifted up and now stood by its hitch rack. The man appeared to be trying to see through the screen door.

"What was that?" Whit said, turning back to Bill finally.

"Now look yere," the boss of the rustlers said, reaching up a big paw which he put on Brand's knee. "Mebbe you don't know who I am. Mebbe where you come from a lot of folks takes you serious, but right around yere you ain't nothin' a-tall. When I ask a straight question I look t' git answered. I ast you — *Dammit!*"

Whit fetched his look back to Bill with a sigh. "Can't we leave this till later?"

It looked like Bill would plumb burst his buttons. A kind of a gurgle came out of his throat and his big fists clenched and whitened his knuckles around the gun and the bottle. Then he said, mighty soft, "Listen yere, pilgrim. If you don't want t' wake up on a cloud with the angels, you pin down yore mind on this talk I'm oratin'. I want t' know how you come t' be with thet dead feller. I want t' know right now — I want t' hear *all about it*. Start spoutin'."

"Oh, that dead feller," Brand said, trying to bring his mind back to it. "I found him sprawled out on a road back yonder."

"What road?"

"Stage road."

"How'd he git that hole in him?"

"That bullet hole?" Whit scratched his

head. "I reckon that stagecoach bunch must of done it. A stage went by not long 'fore I got there. There was a clatter of wheels an' a couple of shots. But when I come to the road there wasn't nothing in sight but this dead feller an' a big cloud of dust boilin' off toward the pass. I reckon this gent tried to hold 'em up. I guess mebbe the guard bored that hole through his brisket."

There wasn't any love light shining in Bill's eyes; they looked considerably jaundiced.

"How good did you look at that dead feller, mister?"

"Pretty good," Whit said, trying to keep up with Bill and watch the Lone Star too. If that girl came out again Whit didn't want to miss her.

"You ever looked over any stiffs before?"

"Some," Whit said.

"What sort of gun would you reckon Mell was killed with?"

"Belt gun, probably. Forty-four or forty-five."

"Then what give you the idea the stage guard shot him?"

Brand looked startled and then surprised. "Say! That's funny —"

"Mell didn't find it funny," Bill snarled. "Buck Tenpott handles the lines on that coach an' Red River Glackey allus rides shotgun fer him. Glackey wouldn't use no belt gun." He reached up a hand. "Lemme look at that hawgleg."

"Say! You ain't thinkin' *I* shot him?"

"Never mind the gab. Pass down that gun!"

"Well," Brand said, "it's a forty-five — but I didn't shoot him. What for would you reckon I'd be wantin' to bore him?"

"If you seen him tryin' t' stick up that stage —"

"But I didn't," Whit said. "First thing I knowed of this feller at all, there he was, face down, in the dust of the road. Jest like what he appears to you now. Not so rumpled up, mebbe, but just as dead."

Curly Bill tried to beat Whit down with his stare. But Whit gave him back a cool look without blinking.

"An' you never seen the shootin'?"

"Time I come up, that stage was along about two mile off an' goin' like they'd make Naco in about ten minutes. It was just at the end of that long grass flat where the road climbs into them rimrocks. Your friend was layin' by that lightnin'-struck pine —"

"Was there anybody in that stage when you seen her?"

28

"I couldn't tell for the dust."

"Do you allow there was?"

"Way this deal stacks up there ain't many choices. If this Glackey didn't shoot him I reckon there must've been. Don't seem like there's no other way to explain it. Unless the driver took a shot at him." Whit looked to see how the big guy was taking it. "Of course," he said, with a sudden thoughtful frown, "if there happened to've been two guys in this stickup —"

"Two!" Curly Bill's black eyes narrowed. "What the hell ever give you that idee?"

"I dunno," Whit said. "It just come over me, sort of. Does that stage get stopped pretty reg'lar?" He squinted at the smoke pouring up from Galey's smelter. "Does she ever haul bullion?"

Curly Bill snorted. "How far would a guy on a horse get with bullion? Only times we ever bother with thet stage is when she's bringin' in the Planchas pay-roll."

"Then I reckon Mell was drilled takin' the payroll off her, or right after he took it off. There's plenty of two-bit crooks in this world that would rather rob robbers than the original owners. Not so much risk gettin' tangled with the law."

"Ride that stretch over."

"Shucks," Whit said, "she's simple enough. Only reason I didn't git onto it right off, the guy must of rubbed his sign out. If Mell didn't have no pardner, somebody else must of knowed about that payroll. This somebody else set back an' let Mell do the grabbin'. All he had to do then was let the stage get away an' put a bullet through Mell an' the Planchas payroll was his for the takin'."

Whit looked at the Lone Star Grub again. He picked up his reins deciding to get over there. "If you're wantin' to auger some more about this —"

"I am," Bill said, "right now!" And before Whit could move, something cold and unbending was shoved against his ribs and he didn't need to look to know the thing was a six-gun. "You an' me," Bill said, "is goin' t' take a little ride. An' we ain't comin' back ontil we git that money!"

3

"BETTER CLIMB
ON THAT HORSE —"

"Don't be a fool," Whit growled, disgusted. "All I been doin' is figurin' it out for you. *I* don't know where that money's got to."

"You'll find it, all right," Bill told him, confident. His teeth flashed out in a wintry smile. "You had better," he added, backing off a few steps and taking another loud swig from the bottle. "Any guy what kin figger as fancy as you been won't hev no trouble over a thing like thet."

He sleeved the beer off his lips and the smile along with it.

"Turn them nags around an' head yonder. An' don't try on no smartness or you're liable t' wake up huggin' a coffin." He grinned again, nastily. "All you got t' do is turn up thet dinero an' you an' me will git along right handsome."

Brand looked at his hole-card and wasn't

encouraged. He had about as much chance as a busted flush. This big galoot with the bandage-wrapped face didn't look quite the kind to stamp and yell boo at; and the offhand way he was wrangling that pistol was enough to make a guy's stomach turn flipflops.

He didn't act like he cared if Whit drew or not!

Whit swore, disgusted, under his breath. He could have choused up a gun fight without coming this far. His own fault, too — Why, a kid still crawling in three-cornered pants would have known a sight better than to fetch in a dead man to this kind of a place!

Suppose he went with this fellow? Suppose they turned up that money? Would this big galoot thank him and call it quits?

Whit took another squint at the guy and felt doubtful. It seemed uncommon likely he would think Whit had hidden it.

Why, the danged fellow looked to be thinking so anyway! There was something downright nasty looking out of those eyes; and cold sweat suddenly broke across Whit's forehead. There was a taunt in that look the big fellow was handing him, a malicious gleam in the flash of those teeth.

He looked as though he'd just as lief

shoot Whit as spit. Whit grabbed hold of himself and breathed carefully. Patience was the password.

The big gent chucked his bottle. He reached up a paw and lifted the .45 out of Whit's holster. He eyed Whit back of it and grinned at him nastily.

Whit didn't like that look.

He twisted his head, slanched a glance toward the Lone Star and, that way, stiffened with his eyes suddenly puckering, forgetting Bill. The shad-bellied man who'd been following Taisy was lounging by the tie rail, thumbs in his gun belt, still watching the screen. There was a man behind that screen door now — Whit could see the guy's back as he stood, half turned, talking over his shoulder, to the girl, most likely. Now the man, still turned and still talking, was pushing open the door.

Whit noticed something then that drove all thought of Curly Bill from his mind. There was another gent easing around the corner of the restaurant, a mustached fellow in a brown derby hat. This guy looked like a Mexican with his sinuous shape, and he was one. It was the Mexican gunman, Emilio Corrado, that Whit had run out of Helvetia some time ago.

The Mexican was lounging there now,

33

propping up the corner, the filled loops of his gun belt shining brightly where the sun lanced across them.

Whit sized up the play and got wise to it pronto. He knew he'd guessed right when he saw Corrado nod to the other man, the shad-bellied one propped against the tie rail. It was a cinch those polecats were laying for someone, and it looked a pretty good bet it was the man in the doorway.

The man pushed open the door.

It was in Whit's mind to shout out a warning, but just as he was fixing to open his mouth Curly Bill snarled about ten inches from his ear: "I'm goin' t' plow me a furrow through thet ivory head of yourn ef you don't turn around an' —"

Whit turned, all right. He turned like a cat swapping ends, and his fetched-up boot took Bill in the chest. The surprised rustler grunted and, as he went rearing back with his arms flying up, Whit snatched at the pistol and wrenched it away from him. He gave a sharp twist and jerked it away and smashed its grip hard against Bill's head.

Curly Bill went down without even a wriggle.

Whit flung his horse around, cutting loose of the gray, and drove the big gelding straight at the Mexican. But so anxious was he to prevent the planned murder, he forgot to turn Bill's pistol around. He was moving too fast to notice that detail and, as his boots struck dirt in a leap from the saddle, the man by the tie rail softly said: "That'll be far enough. Just stop right there."

Whit, twisting a look across his shoulder, froze still as the side of the Whetstone Mountains. No matter how fast he might have moved, the shad-bellied man with the gun would have beat him. It would be swifter to drag a fresh gun into this than to swap his hold on Bill's pistol, which he still held onto by his grip on the barrel. The shad-bellied man had a weapon leveled. He had only to crook his finger. He had only to bend it one fourth of an inch and Whit Brand would find himself strumming a harp. Whit Brand quit moving. He didn't offer any argument.

The man with the drop was a slat-thin gent with a face like burnt leather. He wore checked pants stuffed into his boots and an unbuttoned vest that hung flappily open, disclosing a soiled expanse of boiled shirt. A diamond stud just beneath his string tie caught and threw back the bright rays of the sun. His jaw looked hard as a hoof-shaper's anvil and his cat-yellow eyes were as blank as glass heads.

Whit took a quick look at the derby-hatted Corrado and got a twisted grin from the man's snaky face as the Mexican slid a hand toward the cross-grained grip of his groin-pouched pistol.

Whit's eyes blazed but he kept his lip buttoned.

It was plenty plain this pair of skunks were aiming to kill that gent in the door-way. If only the fellow would look around, if he'd only quit gabbing and realize his danger — it was not yet too late for him to duck back inside.

But the man seemed to have no suspicion of his danger.

Corrado, in his crouch by the building's corner, was all primed and waiting for him to step out in sight.

It seemed incredible anyone could be so brash as to plan a man's death that plain and open right there in broad daylight in the middle of a town. But there wasn't any other very plausible explanation for the looks of this pair or for the way they stood waiting for the man to come out.

A film of sweat again bedewed Whit's brow as the man in the doorway fully opened the screen. He was a frail little gent

in his late fifties with a gray-streaked mustache. He wasn't yet able to see Corrado
when the shad-bellied man in the boiled
shirt said, "Oh, there you are, Colonel — I
was just amblin' over to habla with you.
Oblige me by stepping this way a moment.
There's a couple of —"

"I have nothing to add to what I've already —"

"I know all that — there's been a new
development," Boiled Shirt said, gesturing
toward Brand with the snout of his pistol.
Six men on horseback swept up the street
going hellity-larrup, shouting and shooting
and throwing up dust, but nobody paid
any attention to them. Boiled Shirt said, "I
want you to come down an' look at this
feller."

Brand had seen fright in the colonel's
eyes. He had it hidden now, but the frown
was still twisting his wrinkled cheeks and
the fear was still there, thinly hidden just
behind it.

Whit didn't need any gypsy's crystal to
savvy what Boiled Shirt was up to. In those
few words the man had smoothly estab-
lished a reason for the pistol he held openly
in his hand, and it was all-fired neat how
with those same words he meant to fetch
the colonel out away from that porch where

Corrado would have a good chance to plug him. And when the smoke cleared away it was the man's plain intention for them both to be dead, Whit Brand and the colonel.

"Throw down that gun!" Boiled Shirt snapped curtly.

Whit had plumb forgot he was still holding Bill's pistol.

He let it fall from his hand without argument. But as he dropped the weapon, he started coolly forward, calmly walking toward the muzzle of Boiled Shirt's gun.

Boiled Shirt cursed. He was thrown out of stride by Whit's bold advance. If he fired on Whit, the man he was after, the gray-mustached colonel, would be almost certain to duck back inside. Something of this thinking suddenly showed in his eyes. He couldn't watch Whit and the colonel too, and with Whit walking up to him he had to watch Whit.

By the man's darkening stare Whit could pretty well judge what Boiled Shirt was thinking. The man was locked for that moment in the clash of his urges. Whit had that much respite; it was all he had counted on. He took the last three strides in one jumping lunge.

With a rage-choked snarl the man whipped up his gun. But even as his finger locked round the trigger, Whit Brand's fist struck him flush on the jaw. The gun went off but its charge flew wild. Boiled Shirt measured his length in the gutter.

Even as Whit spun with a frantic hand clawing hard for his armpit, trying to ready himself for attack from the Mexican, a hand grabbed his shoulder and a quick voice said, "You better climb on that horse and get out of here, stranger. That's Marshal Ben Brush you just hung that one on, and I can tell you right now Ben ain't going to like it."

4

SIMON CALLED PETER

The man who had spoken that good advice was got up like the owner of a plantation or a race horse tout, but since there was in that region neither the one nor the other, Wilt Brand didn't quite know what to make of him. There was a distinguished look to his aquiline features and a briskness about him that demanded obedience. A stock at his throat set off the broad shoulders molded smoothly by the expensive fabric of a bottle-green coat. He wore peg-legged trousers and a tall beaver hat, and there was lace at the wrists of his well-cared-for hands.

He was considering Brand with a concerned expression when the colonel, gray-cheeked and mighty obviously frightened, cried, "Thank God!" and shakily gripped the porch rail with both hands.

The man in the bottle-green coat raised his eyebrows. "You know this man, Colonel?"

"I know he just saved my life!" exclaimed the colonel, and the newcomer's eyebrows rose a little higher. His glance roved around with a thoughtful expression, resting briefly on Brush where he lay on his back in the road's yellow dust. Then he looked at Whit Brand and a smile showed his teeth.

"That fist of yours seems to pack quite a wallop. We don't often see Ben Brush where you put him. I'd like to know you better, sir. But right now," he said, withdrawing the smile, "I feel bound to admit that if I were you I would lose no time getting away from here. Our marshal takes himself pretty serious."

Brand nodded. To the colonel he said, "I don't suppose you noticed where that Mexican went?"

The Colonel stared at him blankly.

"A gent named Corrado," Whit told him, and the old man's cheeks went gray again.

The elegant gent in the bottle-green coat said, "Well, I've got to get on — there's a mine owners' meeting I've got to sit in on. Keep your eye peeled, stranger." He waved a smile and departed, going elegantly off up the street toward McConaghey's.

Whit rubbed a hand on his pants

thoughtfully. He was clad in patched over-alls right at the moment and reckoned he must look pretty much like a tramp. Frowning, he looked after the man. The sun-baked dust of the hoof-tracked road erupted little fluffs behind the high-polished boots of the man who had gone to sit in on a meeting. The skallyhooting riders had passed out of sight and the gabbers on the porch of Jack Dall's saloon appeared entirely unaware of the prostrate marshal.

Whit was thinking he ought to get the marshal's gun. Perhaps he ought to help him up and brush him off a little. There was just a vague chance Whit might have misread this thing. It was barely possible the marshal might have had some entirely innocuous reason for calling the old man into the road just then but, remembering Corrado and the colonel's pallor, Brand doubted it.

He looked up to find the man beckoning excitedly.

Whit walked over to the porch and stood there looking up at him. "I ain't askin' no thanks," he said a little grimly. "Just tell me about the guy in the green coat, Colonel. He one of the Foundin' Fathers around here?"

"Lord," declared the colonel, "that's Comstock Kane, boy! Biggest man in these parts, financially speakin'. Mister Kane is the owner of the *Planchas de Oro*."

He breathed the name as though he were speaking of royalty.

Then, abruptly, his look clouded over. "You — really, you've got to get out of this town, my boy — you must go right away." Fright came into his eyes again and they shied nervously away from the disheveled shape of the dust-covered marshal. "Don't think I'm not grateful, my boy — I am. But you've got to get out of here."

"Shucks," Brand said, glancing over at the marshal, "you don't mean on account of him, do you?"

The colonel's wattles quivered. "I most certainly do. That fellow won't rest until Here, let me write you a note."

"No!"

It was the girl's voice — Taisy's.

She stood just behind the old man's shoulder with her head carried proudly and her eyes flashing scorn at Whit. He couldn't think what he had done to warrant such a look, but she left no doubt it was Whit she was looking at. "Don't you do it!" she said to the colonel.

The old man twisted his head for a look

at her. His expression was as bewildered as Whit Brand's own.

"But, my dear," he expostulated, "why the devil shouldn't I?"

Her eyes filled with loathing as they again swept Brand's face. "You were planning to send him out to the mine, weren't you?"

"Yes. I had thought —"

"Well, don't do it!"

"But, Taisy," the old man said, a little nettled, "it's the very least I can do, under the circumstances. This young man's quick thinking just saved my life! At considerable risk —"

"Oh, Dad, don't be such a goon! Can't you *see?*" she cried scornfully. "This is all part and parcel of what happened to Ira. This fine young man —"

"Oh, no! My dear, you're wrong. This young man —"

"Made out to be helping you as a means of establishing himself in your good graces!"

"Taisy!" The colonel's voice was shocked. "You mustn't say such things. You don't know what you're talking about. Brush —"

"I know all about Ben Brush — I heard him," Taisy said. "I can see the whole thing. Brush did nothing whatever except to build up a picture for this ruffian to play to — the whole thing was framed to put you into his indebtedness. I won't have it!" she cried. "It doesn't fool *me!* It's just the slick kind of thing Ben Brush would think of!"

"But the man's a total stranger," the colonel exclaimed. "Surely —"

"Did you suppose Curly Bill would use Crowder or King? Naturally they'd pick a man we hadn't seen before, but I doubt if he's a stranger to anyone but us. If you had seen him drooling over Curly Bill Graham —"

"Curly Bill!" Whit said, startled. "I sure ain't cravin' to contradict no lady, but I don't know Curly Bill from Adam's off ox —"

"Why lie?" Taisy flared. "I saw you talking with him not ten minutes ago! Right over there," she pointed, "under that tree!"

"Good grief!" Whit said. "Was that Curly Bill? That guy in the bandage?"

He looked over there hastily, half reaching for his pistol, but the man he had kicked in the chest had vanished. There wasn't anyone in sight who even vaguely resembled him. Except for the loungers on Jack Dall's porch, the supine marshal and the horses that were tiredly swishing flies at the hitch rails, the street was deserted. That is, practically speaking. There was a woman with a basket entering Shotwell's store. A dog, by the corner, was lifting its leg, but there wasn't any sign of the big burly ruffian with the bandaged face.

"Was *that* Curly Bill?" Whit said again.

"As if you didn't know!"

Even the colonel's faded stare now looked a little dubious.

The girl said to him tartly, "Do you think any man who was a bonafide stranger could have done what this saddle bow slim did to Brush? If that Mexican had really been around, like he claims, would he let a man knock his boss around that way? Look at him!" she said. "Why, he isn't even scared! He looks no more concerned than —"

"I'm considerable concerned, ma'am, that you should be thinkin' so porely of me. For as it happens," Whit said, "I *am* a stranger here. I never seen that guy Brush before in my life, but sure as I'm standin' here him an' that Mex was layin' for the colonel. You can think what you like, but —"

"I shall," she said shortly. "Even if you are a stranger, that's no proof you aren't one of Bill's gang. Nor it isn't any proof

46

you weren't hired for the part you were pretending to play."

There hadn't been much pretense in the way Whit's fist had smacked down the marshal, but he felt in no mood to argue the point. One thing, however, he wanted straight for the record. He wasn't working for anyone and he hadn't come over there to hire out his guns.

He said, "Miz Taisy, ma'am —"

But she wouldn't let him finish. With her eyes flashing a look of triumph at her father, she said, "There's your answer! If this fellow was the stranger he would have us think, how would he happen to know my name?"

Whit stared at her blankly, trapped in his thinking, in that moment too tangled by his own guilty knowledge to remember he had just heard the colonel use it.

But the colonel remembered, and said so. If the remembrance failed to convince the girl, at least it served to renew the old man's faith in him. The girl saw this and flung back her head. "If he's truly so innocent," she said to her father, "why isn't he showing more concern about leaving? Why isn't he frightened or, any rate, worried? Is it normal for a man who has just knocked down a marshal to be standing around looking cool as a well chain? In a town unfamiliar to him — a town run by outlaws? Why isn't he running —"

"Mebbe," Whit said, "I ain't the runnin' kind."

Certain things, certain qualities, were in this girl, and some of these things Whit read in her stare. Pride was in her and a strength of will that would brook no argument. These things were implicit in the way she flung her head back, in the flash of disdain coloring her disbelieving stare. Perhaps it was the measure of her love for her father that made her distrust Whit Brand so thoroughly. Being a charitable man, Whit was willing to concede this; but he was getting riled himself. He was not accustomed to being made out a liar, and he certainly hadn't come all that way to be made out a liar by any chit of a girl, redheaded or otherwise.

He was lifting his hat, intending to take himself elsewhere, when the girl, as though seeing in this an admission of her contentions, said cuttingly: "Run right along — hurry back and tell your bosses that their plan fell through. They will have to get up earlier if they're figuring to fool me."

If she had left it there he would have gone right then, too riled to offer one word

48

in his defense. But, woman-like, she didn't. She had to wring all the juice plumb out of it. She said to her father, "Not even Ben Brush, in all his arrogance, would quite have the gall to kill an unarmed man right here in plain sight of half the town in broad daylight. The whole thing was staged to put this man in our confidence. Come — admit it, Dad. Admit that, for once in my life, I was right."

The colonel looked uncomfortable. But he shook his head. "You are often right, Taisy, but you're wrong about this. The boy may have been mistaken, but he certainly thought he was saving my life. You didn't see Brush's eyes — you didn't see Corrado —"

"Did *you?*"

"I didn't see Corrado, no; but I believe he was there and —"

"Oh, Dad!" Taisy cried, as though she found the notion intolerable.

"The very least I can do," the colonel said doggedly, "is to help this young man."

"You don't need to worry about *me,*" Whit scowled, giving the girl back look for look. "I expect I can make out to take care of myself."

"I feel sure of it," Taisy said, smiling with false sweetness.

But the colonel had dug up a notebook and pencil and was now bent forward industriously writing. He tore out the page and put the book in his pocket. "This isn't an act of charity," he said, extending the paper as though he meant Brand to take it. "I need a man to go out to the Luckybug and you'll find the directions — What'd you say your name was?"

"Brand," Whit said, "but —"

"All right, Brand! Git them dew-claws up!" a tight voice harshly bade from behind him; and Brand knew his luck had at last run out. While he'd stood there hearing himself maligned by the girl whose picture had brought him into this, the shad-bellied marshal had come to and taken over.

From the corners of his eyes Whit could see him getting up. He might still be some confused in his mind, but there was nothing confused about his grip on that smokepole. He had its snout blackly focused on Whit Brand's middle and the look of his face said he'd just as well use it.

Whit put his hands up.

"There! You see?" Taisy smiled, wheeling round on her father. "Do you think Ben Brush would act so mild with a stranger? He's just what I said he was, a cheap drifting gunslick Bill has picked up — a saddle bow slim that will stoop to anything just so he gets the wage his treacherous acts have earned him! Can you doubt it now — *can* you? He's the same breed of rat as the rest of these ruffians."

That was all Whit heard.

The rest was blanked out in a burst of bright lights. He felt his knees buckling. He saw the ground coming up. He went down a long spiral that got blacker and blacker.

5

JUST A CHEAP CROOK

Brand opened his eyes on a rough plank ceiling in a dusty room with two doors and a window. Its battered and spur-gouged furnishings were entirely on the practical side; two chairs put together with hide by an Indian, a roll-top that looked like it had come over on the Ark and an old two-gallon wooden bucket with a bailing-wire handle.

Boiled Shirt lounged against the deck — Boiled Shirt Brush, the Galeyville marshal, who had aimed to shoot down an unarmed man in broad daylight. Corrado, his trigger man, derby hat tipped forward to shade his glinting eyes, was hunkered on his boot heels alongside the window. Both had their gaze pinned unwinkingly on Brand, who was gradually discovering that his face was wet, that his back was on the floor in a puddle of water.

He also discovered that his head hurt

and that the room whirled crazily every time he moved.

He climbed onto his feet without remark and stood swaying.

"Feelin' better?" Brush asked.

Brand looked at him dourly. "What's the charge?" he said finally.

"We're waitin'," Brush said, "for Mister Graham to file one."

Whit thought about that and wished his head would quit banging. "Do I know Mister Graham?"

"He'll know *you*, all right," Brush dug a toothpick out of his pocket, stuck it in his mouth and stood chomping it thoughtfully while his unblinking stare coldly roved over Brand's features. "Can't figure how come you to mix into this. Who sent fer you?"

Brand sighed. "An' that's the thanks I get for tryin' to help you out. Hadn't been for me you'd be strummin' a harp on some pink cloud by this time. I done what any gent would of done when I seen this guy by the corner with his gun out. I figured he was liftin' that gun to bore you. It sure looked to me like you was goin' to be a goner if I didn't get you out of the way in a hurry. So I socked you. An' for that you bend a gun on my scalp."

Brush nodded. "Case of misunderstandin' all around, it looks like. I seen him, myself, about the time I come to I seen he had a gun out an' that's why I tapped you. Kind of hard light to judge by — couldn't tell who he was fer a second. Turns out he's my deputy." The marshal took out his toothpick and elaborately examined it before shoving it back between his yellow teeth again. "Ever been here before?"

Brand was tenderly feeling of the bump on his head. He didn't have to feel for his pistols. He saw all three of them piled upon the desk.

"Ever been here before?" Brush repeated.

"No."

"Reckon somebody sent fer you. Ol' Man Wainright?"

Whit didn't answer.

Brush said, "What was you doin' with the Wainright dame's picture?"

"So you been through my pockets, have you?" Brand said, scowling.

"That's a habit we got, goin' through pris'ners' pockets. Now look" — Brush said — "I'm a patient man. I try to guide myself by the Golden Rule. But when I chuck out a question I like to get answered. What was you doin' with the Wainright dame's picture?"

"I found it," Brand frowned.

There was a moment of silence. The kind of quiet that abounds before the first thunderclap.

"He found it," Brush said to Corrado.

The Mexican grinned.

Brush said to Whit, "I find that kind of remarkable." He continued to study Brand another several moments. "I guess you found McLown's wallet. Did you find Smith's letters?"

Whit nodded. He wished right away that he hadn't. The room twirled round like Uncle Lively.

When it rocked back to focus Ben Brush said grimly, "Mind tellin' me where?"

Whit couldn't see where this was heading but it seemed unlikely any good would come of it. "What's all that got to do with my bein' here?"

"That's what I'm tryin' to find out," Brush said. "Whereabouts did you find them?"

"I found them on a dead feller in the Santa Ritas."

"That's a long walk from here. Guess you come to return 'em."

Brand didn't see as how that called for any answer.

"I been weaned quite a spell," Brush

mentioned casually, and for another few moments the silence hung heavy. Brush went to the door and spit out his toothpick. He came back and sat on a corner of the desk.

"Who sent fer you?" he said.

"There didn't nobody send for me."

Brush searched his pockets till he found another toothpick. He put it in his mouth and chewed the end of it awhile.

"I been tryin' to be nice to you, mister."

He let Whit consider that a spell and then he said: "You ready to talk?"

Maybe Brand's mind wasn't working so good. The marshal looked at the Mexican. Corrado got up and came to stand beside Whit.

"Who sent for you?" Brush said.

"I told you. Nobody sent for me."

Corrado said, "Look!" and shoved out his left hand. When Whit looked down at it the Mexican hit him.

Whit woke up on the floor and the puddle of water appeared to have grown bigger. He seemed to have got his face in it somehow.

The marshal helped him up. He brushed Whit off and handed him his hat again. "You want to watch where you're goin'. You want to be more careful, Slim.

This floor's pretty slippery. You might hurt yourself fallin' around on it that way."

Whit glared groggily and wished to hell the room would stand still awhile.

He sleeved the water off his chin and got the room into focus.

"What fetched you over here?" Ben Brush said.

Whit was tempted to tell him it was none of his business, but better judgment won out. "If you got to know," he growled, hot and scowling, "I come over to get a look at that girl in the picture."

The marshal considered him for quite a long while. "Well, it could be," he mused. "I suppose it could, anyway. Young Lochinvar, eh?"

Whit could tell by his look the marshal didn't believe him.

Brush looked at Corrado. "It don't seem like this feller's very bright in the head. Maybe if he was to fall down again . . ."

The Mexican grinned. He looked at his fist and then looked at Whit Brand.

Whit said, "You asked me," and the marshal nodded.

"Try the truth for a change."

"I told you the truth!"

The marshal looked to Corrado. "I

guess," Brush said, "he don't understand kindness."

Corrado stepped around the bucket. He stopped in the puddle about a foot from Brand.

"If you try that again," Whit said through tight lips, "you'll be wishin' you never was borned!"

Brush picked up one of the guns off the desk. He twirled it around on a finger, smiling. "I wouldn't do nothin' brash," he said.

While the marshal and Whit were eyeing each other, and the derby-hatted Mexican was eyeing his fist, the door banged open and Curly Bill came in.

He stopped with a clank of his big-roweled spurs. He looked at the still dripping front of Brand's shirt, at the puddled floor and Brand's swelling face.

"What the hell's comin' off here?" he said to Ben Brush.

"We're gettin' his statement," the marshal said mildly. "You figurin' to prefer any charges?"

Curly Bill slewed his tongue across thick lips. His bloodshot eyes roved over Brand.

He said without taking his eyes off Whit, "I shore can't figger this pilgrim noways. I reckon you heard, Ben, what the driver of

that stage an' the shotgun guard said —
how a black-masked feller stuck up the
stage an' made off with the Planchas mine
payroll? You reckon this jigger could of
done it?"

"I expect he could of," Brush said
noncommittally.

"I sent Mell Snyder out t' do thet job.
This feller comes in packin' Snyder's body.
Claims he found Mell dead out alongside
the road. What do you make of a yarn like
that?"

"He's quite a finder," Brush said, and
grinned sourly. "Whereabouts along the
road?"

"By thet lightnin'-struck pine."

"Well, it don't seem too likely but it
could of been so." Brush thought a while
and then he said to Bill, "Mell could of let
it get out what he was up to. He could of
told some friend. The friend could of told
someone else. Mebbe the friend decided to
cut himself in on it. He might of let Mell
take the money off the stage an' then
throwed down on Mell and salted him.
Mebbe Mell double-crossed you — mebbe
someone crossed up Mell. A lot of things
could of happened."

"What do you think happened?"

"Well," Brush said, "I would lay my bet

this saddle bow slim here come along about the time Mell was doin' his business. I figure he prob'ly hid out in the bushes till Mell got the payroll an' the stage drove off. Then this slick gent kills Mell an' grabs the payroll."

Curly Bill took another gloating look at Brand's face.

"While you're at it," Brand said, "tell him how I lugged off all that coin."

"How do you know how much coin there was?"

"There musta been a pile if there was enough to fetch two road-agents after it."

"Unless you're countin' yourself, no one's said there was two," Brush murmured. There was wicked glee in his bead-bright stare. "An' you, bein' the second one, had sure ought to know!"

Whit said to Curly Bill, "A payroll would be packed in the stage company's strong-box. What did this guy have to pack it off on? Did he reckon to tie it onto his saddle?"

Curly Bill's glance narrowed. "I guess he had a extry horse."

"Funny what become of it then," Whit said. "The only bronc I could find was the one I packed him in on, an' I looked around pretty good," Whit told Bill. "I sure didn't turn up no strong-box, neither, nor any sign of a mark where it hit the ground. Go on out an' look for yourselves; don't take my word."

Curly Bill and Ben Brush exchanged glances. Brush said disinterestedly, "That's a job fer Johnny Behan. I ain't concerned with what goes on in the county." He said to Curly Bill, "This sport probably buried it."

"Then you ought to be able to find it," Whit said. "I didn't have no shovel an' no feller my size would be luggin' a strong-box any further'n you could spit. If I'd hid it I'd of had to drag it, an' draggin' leaves marks —"

"Your horse could of drug it," Brush said, smiling nastily. "An' there wasn't nothin' stoppin' you from cuttin' yourself a greasewood switch an' dustin' out any marks it left."

Curly Bill was watching Whit's face intently. "You may git away with that money," he said, "but you sure as hell won't spend none of it."

A watch in somebody's pocket beat against the stillness. Whit saw Bill's fists clench. He caught the hard glint of Corrado's eyeballs, saw the way the blue shirt stretched across Bill's chest.

A smile was lallygagging across Brush's mouth and Whit was mightily tempted to make a pass at him and to heck with the consequences; but it was that kind of impulse that had trapped him like he was right now. If he hadn't been so danged impulsive he wouldn't ever have come to this town in the first place.

He got a hold on his temper, well knowing the only chance he had was what little chance his wits might devise for him. About the only chance he could see right then was for a mighty short life and an unknown grave.

He said to Bill earnestly: "I told you the truth — Snyder was dead when I found him. There was a black bandanna tied across his face an' his gun was layin' about a foot from his hand with the muzzle jammed full of dirt. I heard his horse whinnyin' off in the brush. I fetched it an' loaded him on. I figured he'd tried stickin' up the stage an' some guy aboard her had bored him. But just in case I was wrong I looked around anyhow. I cut for sign all around that place but —"

"If he'd been shot from the stage," Ben Brush put in, "there'd be a hole in him big enough to drive a team through. When Glackey rides he don't use no pistol. He packs a sawed-off Greener for that kind of work —"

"I didn't say Glackey shot him," Whit flared. "I don't know who shot him, except it sure wasn't me. Some gent inside —"

"That stage come in three hours ago. There wasn't nobody on it but the guard an' the driver, an' nothin' inside it but a couple of sacks of ore specimens Kane was gettin' back from the Tucson assayer's office."

"That don't prove I done it!"

"Don't it?" Brush said. "I talked to them fellers. They throwed off the box an' —"

"Look," Whit said to Bill desperately. "I been marshalin' Helvetia, as this Mex here can tell you. Would I come all this way just to stick up —"

"What *did* you come here fer?" Brush demanded, quick suspicion in his voice. And the rustler boss nodded, darkly probing Whit's features.

Whit heaved a sigh and shrugged his shoulders. It didn't make any difference what he told these fellows. They wouldn't believe him on a stack of bibles. There would be no use telling Bill the truth, how he'd come over there on account of a picture. Bill'd never believe a gent to be that loco.

"Make it good while you're at it," Brush said with a sneer.

Whit looked at him bitterly but didn't say anything.

Brush swung his face toward Curly Bill. "I'm goin' to tell you somethin' before you waste any more of your time on this feller. He's just a cheap crook with a fast line of gab."

He went over to the roll-top and picked up something. "I don't know how much you know about him, but I've uncovered a couple of things myself. He gives out he's been marshalin' the town of Helvetia. Take a look at this here an' see what *you* think. It's somethin' I just got out of his pocket."

It was something, all right. Ben Brush wasn't lying.

Whit took one look and his guts started crawling.

The thing Ben Brush was holding out to Bill was the wallet with *Ira McLown* stamped on it. The wallet Whit had got the girl's picture out of. The wallet he had taken off Stampede Smith.

6

BRUSH BARES HIS TEETH

Whit could tell that wallet was poison to him by the quiet way Bill eyed it, by the malicious laughter that looked out of Brush's stare.

He watched the rustler boss turn it over and felt his stomach turn over with it. You couldn't tell what Bill was thinking but it plainly forecast nothing good to Whit's health. He stood tapping the wallet on the fingers of his left hand, considering Whit without expression. "McLown's," he said, and passed it back.

The marshal's lips peeled off his teeth.

He gave Curly Bill a knowing nod. "That's right," he said. "It's the wallet McLown put his mine-sale money in just before he left Kane's house that night. The wallet McLown was robbed of as he came down the steps of Shotwell's store. The same wallet, Bill."

He looked at Whit smugly and stood

back with arms folded.

"All right," Bill said. "What are you drivin' at, Ben?"

"This cheap crook says he ain't never been in this country before."

Curly Bill turned his head and looked at Whit's face narrowly. There were things in that stare which were hard to get straight, but the suspicion it held was not one of them.

Brush said, his voice soft with malice, "Ask him where he got it, why don't you?"

Bill was looking at Whit with a face that was growing more baffled. There was a vexed frown on it and his eyes were queer, too. They were puzzled.

"What the hell'd you come back fer?" he asked Whit finally.

Brand shrugged and Corrado commenced rubbing his fist. He lifted his knuckles and blew on them slyly and the marshal's cat eyes shone brighter and brighter.

Whit planted his feet more solidly under him. Unaccountable tensions flowed through the room like currents of air curling up from a rat hole.

Curly Bill said querulously, "I don't git this — by cripes, I don't git no part of it."

Whit expected him to put the question

Brush had suggested and was wondering why Brush had wanted it asked, but the big burly rustler started prowling the room, started clanking his big-roweled spurs around in the saddle-cramped swagger that seemed his natural gait.

He stopped with his eyes brightly fixed on the marshal. "There's somethin' damn fishy about this whole deal. Why would Kane give McLown a thousand smackers for nothing?"

"You got to remember," Brush said, "it wasn't exactly for nothin'. Kane paid him that money for McLown's half-interest in the Luckybug Mine."

"Yeah," Bill said with curling lip. "Fer McLown's half-interest to a hole in the ground! Wainright ain't got no mine an' never did hev, an' Comstock Kane knows it! I don't believe he ever give him that money!"

"Well, he did," Brush said. "I went up there an' asked him. That's exactly what he done. He give him one thousand dollars in foldin' money."

"Then he done it fer somethin' else," Bill growled. "You can't tell me no man in his senses —"

"The point," Brush said, "is that he give him the money. He seen McLown stuff it away in this wallet. McLown went from Kane's straight to Shotwell's store. Set aroun' there gabbin' for the balance of the evenin'."

"An' never opened his trap about Kane or the money!"

"I can't help that. The fact is he done it." The marshal's cat-yellow eyes stared unblinkingly. He seemed to gauge Bill's reactions before Bill had them. Slick, that's what Brush was — slick as slobbers. "He never opened his mouth about that deal. Yet the very minute he steps out of Shotwell's store this cheap crook here rams a gun in his ribs an' —"

"Why, you forked-tongued liar!" Whit yelled. He started for Brush to ram the words down his throat but Bill flung him back and took the play away from him.

"You don't know thet, Ben," Bill said. "You're jest guessin'."

"Want to try your hand?" Brush said, smiling easy. "A guy that'll steal a horse will do anything." And he gave Bill back look for look, like a panther. "Mebbe you didn't happen to notice, but this guy rode in here leadin' O'Dade's gray. The one he works with his mule on that scraper — that flea-bit gray stud horse."

"I bought that horse!"

"Let's see your bill of sale."

Whit rammed an angry fist in his pocket, but he knew before his fingers found the pocket empty that O'Dade's bill of sale wouldn't be there. He knew it by the gleam in the marshal's eyes. He said: "You chiseling crook —"

"Never mind that," Bill said impatiently. His black eyes snapped back to Brush again. "If this guy robbed McLown I guess McLown would recogn—"

"It was dark," Brush said. "McLown didn't even get a look at the guy. He stepped out of the store an' somethin' hit him."

"Just the same," Bill said doggedly, "if this guy done it, Kane put him up to it."

Brush shrugged his shoulders. "I don't know nothin' about that. I'm no politician. I hev to deal with facts. An' the facts is that now, jest a couple weeks later, this feller turns up with Pat O'Dade's horse, Snyder's dead body and McLown's empty wallet."

Framed neat as a picture! Whit thought bitterly. He had put their noose right around his neck when he'd come busting in there with those three items.

His face was a picture of angry confusion, but Bill never noticed. He was eyeing

Ben Brush. His big shoulders were hunched and his huge fists doubled. He had thought a lot faster than Whit had given him credit for. He said, "Ben, if you're headed where you look t' be —"

"I ain't headed no place. I'm statin' the facts."

"You're as good as sayin' Mell Snyder grabbed that money!"

"Take your pick," Brush said. "Mell Snyder or this guy."

"The man who grabbed that money," Whit told them, "was a feller so narrer he could bathe in a gun barrel. A red-faced southpaw in a —"

"Smith, by Gawd!"

There was something ugly in the way Bill said that. The look he fixed on the marshal was the kind no man could be expected to stand for, but the marshal spread steady hands in a shrug.

"You stop to reflect for a minute," he said, "an' you'll begin to see how this thing really looks. Here's a guy claims he ain't never been here before, yet all the signs an' signal smokes goes to prove he's lyin'."

He said to Bill smoothly, "Consider these facts," and ticked them off, as he talked, on his fingers. "He comes in this mornin' on a horse O'Dade tells me was

70

stole from him — Pat O'Dade — last week. This guy claims he bought the horse from O'Dade, but he can't show nothin' to back it up. He's packin' McLown's wallet which he says he *found*. Now he tells us Smith grabbed it, an' he knows what Smith looks like. He knows Taisy Wainright — he was packin' her picture — an' he heads for Wainright's first thing he hits town. Don't ask where to find him, just heads right for him like a steer heads for water."

He wrinkled his nose with a show of disgust. "He'll prob'ly be tellin' us next how it was Mister Kane that put Smith up to it. Land's sakes, Bill!" His lips curled back in a scathing grin. "I would think you'd have more savvy, by grab, than to lap up that kind of hogwash."

Curly Bill's fat cheeks went dark and twisted. He turned bleak eyes on Whit, and the cords in his flushed neck were tight and swollen.

Whit's thoughts whirled desperately round and round, seeking some out, some way to squeeze past the marshal's slick talk. But there wasn't any way. The marshal's words were damning.

Whit said, "I found that wallet on Smith's dead body. It was about ten days ago, up in the Ritas. I was after a guy that

71

had stuck up a deadfall. I was gettin' pretty close, accordin' to the sign. I heard horses suddenly; their sound was comin' up out of a gully. I figured the guy I was trailin' had met up with some friends. I laid back a while, thinkin' them others would dust; but when the guns started spoutin' I dug for there pronto. Where I come up on the gully there was a overhangin' ledge that kept me from seein' what was happening down there. It took me a spell to find a way down. I had to ride a few miles before I could get down into it.

"It was evenin', and by the time I got down there, it was gettin' dark fast. It was this Smith; he was dead when I found him. Them fellers hadn't wasted no time an' was gone. I rode after 'em a ways, hopin' to come up with them, but they was diggin' for the tules an' not pickin' no daisies. I went back to Smith. I found that empty wallet on him an' a couple of letters — That's how I knew what his name was."

"An' the picture," Brush sneered. "Don't forget the picture."

"The picture," Whit said, "was in the wallet. It was stuck way down in one corner. It had a girl's name on it. 'Taisy,' it said."

Brush held out the picture to Bill.

72

The rustler boss took it with a hard look at Brand.

"I don't see no name," Brush said, "do you?"

Whit stared across Curly Bill's shoulder. There was no name on it. The picture's back was blank.

"So how the hell," Brush said, "did he know what her name was?"

"Where's the letters?" Bill said, and Brush shook his head. "He didn't have no letters — not that I could find. There's the rest of the stuff I took off him, right there on the desk. Three guns, about eight hundred dollars in foldin' money, this picture an' that wallet. Ask Corrado. He was right here with me."

Silence closed over that room, tight and ugly.

Hot words pounded Whit's teeth, struggling for utterance, but Whit choked them back. There was nothing he could say that would change this picture Ben Brush had painted. Brush had paid him back for that punch in good measure. Brush had done everything but put the rope round his neck. If he'd thought it necessary he'd have done that, too.

Whit wondered why Bill had gone so thoughtfully quiet. Bill stood there with his blacksmith's shape turned still and unmoving.

Brush said with sly malice, "Don't look like she'd of give her picture to no total stranger. Don't look like no stranger would be knowin' which stage was packin' the Planchas payroll, neither, nor where Mell Snyder was figurin' to stop it."

Whit looked at him sharply. He had thought all the time Brush had been framing him, but it came over him now it was a much bigger loop this crooked marshal had been twirling.

Curly Bill said thinly: "So you've got him workin' fer me now, hev you? Let me tell you, I never got one penny from that stuck-up stage — nor out of that damn' wallet, neither!"

Brush laughed shortly. "You sure make a pile of dust about it. I recall you always was noisy," he said. "Mostly I try to get along with folks, but don't hug the notion I'm scared of you, Bill. My bread's bein' buttered by this camp's solid citizens. John H. Galey an' some other folks round here is gettin' plenty tired of your paw an' beller. You better pull in your horns if you want to stay healthy."

Brand looked for the outlaw to blast Brush down. His big chest swelled like he

74

would bust his surcingle. His face got roan as a stuck pig's throat and his eyes looked like they would roll off his cheekbones.

They didn't, however, and his voice when he spoke was like it came through velvet. Perhaps the gun Brush picked up had something to do with the pitch of Bill's voice, the way it crept from his teeth like a spider's footfalls.

He said, "You better be recallin' who you owe fer that job." And he didn't say one other word — not one.

7

"SO YOU'RE GOING
TO PLAY DUMB, EH?"

When he'd gone Brush went over and shut the door.

He did it like he'd just thrown an armful of trash out. He wiped his hands on his pants and gave a hitch to his gun belt.

Corrado tramped over and sat on the desk, swinging his legs and watching Brand, grinning.

Brush looked at Whit slanchways.

Whit didn't like that look at all, not the tone of Brush's voice when the marshal said grimly, "I guess you know where you stand now, don't you?"

Whit grinned at him sourly. "If you're through with me now —"

"I ain't hardly got started," Brush informed him dryly, and stood there a while coldly studying Brand's face.

Brush said, "Don't you like it here?"

"I been places I liked better."

"That'll be nice to look back on," Brush said without smiling. "You should of thought about that before you come rompin' over here. Man that shoves his chips in another gent's game is sure askin' for whatever he gets. You ain't tough — you only think you are. I've met a pile of your kind an' I'm still in the saddle."

His voice changed abruptly; its edge grew sharper. "If you want to get out of this mess, start talkin'. Who asked you into this, Bill or Wainright?"

Whit wished he'd stayed plumb away from that camp. He thought of all the good times behind him, the hard times too, the folks he had known. He had never before come across a guy like Brush. There was a cunning in Brush that both enraged and alarmed him. The man was quiet as a spider, about as devious, too. He had played with Bill like a spider with a fly. With Curly Bill, the acknowledged king of the owlhoots, a fellow most tough gents were glad to steer clear of.

That told Whit something. It told Whit the marshal must have powerful backing. Was it Kane? Was it Galey that stood behind Brush?

Not Galey, Whit thought. John Galey

was straight. He wouldn't be used by a crooked marshal; he wouldn't fool round with him. Galey was a miner, the man who founded that hell-roaring town, the man who had discovered the first silver in those hills. He wasn't the kind to get mixed up in politics. Whit would have staked his shirt politics was in this. Someone was out to get control of the camp. Bill bossed it now, or was reputed to boss it. Someone was out to put his knife in Bill and this crooked marshal was helping him.

That was Whit's thought, but he didn't say so. He didn't say anything.

Ben Brush's yellow eyes kept digging at him, prodding him. "Was it Bill or Wainright?"

Whit scowled at the gun hanging loose in Brush's fist, at the gleeful grin on the face of Brush's deputy. It would not be Corrado this time, he thought. It would be that gun Brush was languidly waving.

A gun was more permanent. A gun could be final.

"What are you cravin' to have me say?"

"The truth," Brush smiled. "It was Wainright, wasn't it?"

"I don't know any Wainright."

Brush said with a rasp: "Are a handful of words worth gettin' yourself killed for?"

His yellow eyes held the look of a crouching wild thing, but he pulled his voice down and said more quietly, "The quicker you talk the quicker you'll be done with this."

Corrado got off his perch on the desk and warily came toward Whit.

"Pore Sleem," he said with a gusty sigh. "No poppa, no momma, pretty soon no more Sleem." The mechanical smile glinted under his mustache.

A sullen anger colored Whit's cheeks.

"You better talk," Brush said. "Think it over, kid. I'll give you another couple minutes." He stood back, and dug out a toothpick which he stuck in his mouth and proceeded to munch on while his bleached yellow stare continued to probe Whit's face.

"I'll find out anyway," he said. "I got ways. If you got any wheels in that thinkbox, kid, you better start usin' 'em while you're able."

"You wouldn't dare —"

"Wouldn't *what?*" Brush licked his chops and said mildly, "You wouldn't be the first crook I shot escapin'. All you've done has been to make me trouble. I want the truth out of you an' I want it pronto."

"I told you the truth. I don't know no Wainright."

Corrado edged closer.

"When I asked you where you got the Wainright dame's picture you savvied quick enough what I was talkin' about. Now get this kid, an' get it quick. That skinny old jasper you seen at the Lone Star is the girl's ol' man — Colonel Jim Wainright. I want to know when he sent for you, an' why."

"Him?" Brand said. "That guy you called the colonel? That's Wainright? Hell, I didn't know him from Adam. I seen this Corrado sport layin' for him —"

"The truth," Brush hinted gently.

"I'm givin' you the truth! I didn't know that was Wainright — wouldn't of meant nothin' to me if I had. I never heard of him before. I didn't know this Mexican was one of your deputies; I run him out of Helvetia a couple months ago. How would I know you made him a deputy? Why, cripes," Whit said, "I didn't know you was a marshal till after I'd knocked you skedaddlin'."

Brush nodded slowly. "All right," he said. "It must of been Curly Bill. What did Bill get you up here for? What did he tell you?"

"I never seen Bill Graham."

"You didn't have to see him. He could of sent you word."

"I told you once what it was brought me up here. I come here," Whit said, "to get a look at that girl."

"And how did you know that girl was up here?"

"From that picture an' the letters I took off Smith. . . ."

Whit quit, disgusted. He could wear out his voice and not tell Brush anything. The marshal was sold on the notion Whit was lying.

"So you want to be stubborn. So you're goin' to play dumb, eh?"

Corrado grabbed Whit's arm and doubled him over with a twist of it. His garlicky breath was hot in Whit's face, his lips were stretched in a grin just behind it.

"I take care of these feller! I make heem talk."

"Yeah," Brush said. "He don't appreciate a feller tryin' to be nice to him. Lock him up, Corrado. You can play with him later."

8

CONVERSATIONAL

Back of the counter in the Lone Star Grub old Colonel Jim Wainright was pouring himself a whisky, but half the time it never hit the glass. Not even the sun flashing through the clean windows could make his drawn cheeks appear less gray. He was a man badly rattled, he was a man plainly scared.

He was muttering to himself and there was a dreadful expression staring out of his eyes. "Them fellers was fixing to kill me, Taisy! Brush an' that Mexican he's got for a deputy — I never seen Brush so mad in my life as he was when that young feller busted his play up! They was sure fixed to do it. They was all set an' waitin' for me to step out that door!"

"But that's ridiculous, Dad!"

Taisy's cheeks hardly backed up her talk; they were almost as pale as the old man's gray ones. But the look of her eye and the vigorous way she laid out her words showed the turn she wished her thought to take.

"No one would ever consider Brush an angel, but only a fool — and I'm sure he's not that — would dare attempt plain murder in broad daylight. It's preposterous! The whole town knows you never carry a gun —"

"The whole town knows Curly Bill runs this camp an' that Brush is Bill's man," the colonel said doggedly. He shook his head and reached again for the bottle. "I'm tellin' you, Taisy, them fellers aimed to kill me. I reckon they had some plan cooked up to clear themselves. . . . But I saw that look in Brush's eyes just as plain — why, if it wasn't for that young feller horning in —"

"Good Lord," Taisy said, "that's what they wanted you to think! Oh, Dad — can't you see? The whole thing was cooked up just to make you feel indebted to that fellow!"

"Then they done a good job. Nothin'll ever convince me that I wouldn't be dead if it hadn't been for that young feller pitchin' in when he did. I sure feel beholden to him."

Taisy stamped her foot and clenched her

hands, frowning angrily. With that color in her cheeks she looked prettier than ever. Yet, even so, exasperated as she was at her father's refusal to admit her right, she was more scared than mad. It was this ragged fear that made her so emphatic. "When you started working the Luckybug, everybody laughed at you. Wainright's Folly, they called it — remember? Even Mister Kane, that you set so much store by, told you the thing was no better than a pocket."

"He said —"

"Of course! I know what he said. He said it *might* pan out, but he never really thought so. You know he didn't. He was letting you down easy — keeping up a fiction on account of me."

She blushed furiously, tossed her head and went on. "There was no ore in place and never has been. It's been three months now since you even had color."

"But I'll have it. You just wait a bit. You just wait," declared the colonel, with his eyes glinting like the eyes of all burro men. "One of these days I'll —"

"Find another pocket!" Taisy cried irritably, and was repentant as soon as she said it. She wasn't a heartless girl — not a bit of it. Youth and impatience had spawned those words, exasperation had

84

given voice to them. She loved her father but she couldn't help rebelling at the man's blind faith. Too many years of rainbow chasing had shown her how mistaken he was. The hard life they'd led was what killed her mother, worn her out before her time. *One of these days I'll strike it rich!* How many times had she heard that cry, that clarion call of all burro men, that eternal hope of all prospectors. It was their faith, their credo. *One of these days I'll strike it rich!* It was always going to be the next shovelful, the next rock tapped, the next pan washed. The next day's sunset would find them rich. The mañana of the Mexicans, the tomorrow that never came.

"Never mind," Taisy said, choking back her rebellion, "we'll make out some way. . . ."

"Yes — yes, of course," agreed the old man eagerly. "Just a little more time. Just another ten feet. That drift —" His faded eyes gleamed, and he was off in the glorious world of Discovery, unearthing the pot at the foot of the rainbow, turning up a bonanza, aglow at his finds. "Yes, of course," he said, picking up his hat.

Roused again, with her eyes gone anxious, Taisy put out a hand. "You're not going out to the mine again now?"

"But Taisy, I've got to! I'm almost onto it. Look!" he cried, digging a fist down into his pocket. "Look at this, by godfreys!" He held out a rock fragment, thrust it toward her with a shaking hand. "I guess that's just float! Mebbe it ain't jewelry, but it's plenty good enough for a starter!"

Taisy stared at it. It *was* ore — good ore, too. Even Taisy's inexperienced eyes could tell that much. "Where did you find it?"

"I guess that's pocket stuff!" the old man cackled. "Wait'll Com Kane sees that, by jingoes!"

Taisy sighed resignedly. There would be no curbing him now for a while. She knew as she passed the specimen back to him they were going to be in for another of his wild bursts of energy. It took no more than that to set him off. He would think, eat and drink, even dream bonanza until this streak played out as all the others had.

Taisy tried to smile. Her heart ached for him. "It's the ledge, you think?"

"I dunno," he said, turning cagey. "Ain't got far enough into it to tell yet — only broke that piece off yesterday. I'll say this much, though: it *looks* like the ledge — it *looks* like the same stuff the Planchas is producing."

86

Taisy thought despairingly of past enthusiasms. "But you're not even close to Kane's *Planchas de Oro*. There are two claims nearer, two claims between the Luckybug and —"

"Which I've bought," said the colonel, not at all dashed by that.

Yes, she thought, with his usual profligacy he had dipped his hands deep into the savings she had wrung from the restaurant to buy these claims which the smarter Kane had considered worthless. And even these weren't anywhere near the Planchas tunnel; they were closer than the Luckybug, but they were not near. Kane had claims of his own that were nearer.

She said, "Why do you suppose Kane bought out Ira's interest?"

Old Jim looked impatient. "He told us why he bought Ira out. Ira was busting to sell, as you very well know. *We* couldn't buy him out. Comstock took Ira's half as a means of protecting us. Suppose Curly Bill —"

"I could almost wish he had," Taisy sighed. "At least we would know where we stood in that case."

The old man shook his head. "I can't understand why you've never liked Comstock. He's the best friend we've got in this camp, Taisy. If it wasn't for him and John Galey. . . ."

Taisy shrugged. She didn't quite know herself why she didn't like Kane. In his immaculate clothes and with his handsome features and distinguished air — the richest man in these parts if you could believe the stories — she should have thought him a good catch. Other girls did and made no bones about it. Why, that girl from the Three Bars, Kettie Farron —

Taisy blushed. She said quickly, "I'd like to shake Ira's teeth out! He might at least have let us know. We might have somehow managed to. . . ."

The old man downed another slug of his whisky. He drove the cork in the bottle and put it away. His cheeks took on a little more color. He set down the glass and patted Taisy's shoulder. "Just because a man wants to marry you, honey —"

"I wouldn't marry Kane if —"

"Well, well, you don't have to," old Jim said hastily. "You certain sure don't have to. But you can't keep the feller from hoping."

"We're getting off the subject," Taisy said, steering the talk back. "What I started to say was that it's all of a pattern, Kane buying out Ira and now this drifter showing up and trying to make himself

88

solid with a cooked up scheme to make you think he saved your life. Why do you suppose," she asked suddenly, "Kane closed down the Planchas?"

"I told you why he closed it. He's taken a firm stand against the lawlessness round here. He refused to operate for the benefit of road-agents. No man or company can go on losing payrolls."

"That's his story."

"Of course it's his story," the colonel said indignantly. "It's the truth! You know Curly Bill's bunch have been sticking that stage up."

"They could have put on more guards — he could have put guards of his own on. Nothing to stop him from doing that, was there? He could have complained to Sheriff Behan."

"He has. Johnny Behan can't police the whole country!"

"It looks queer to me," Taisy said, unconvinced. "Kane closes his mine, one of the camp's best producers, posts guards around it and pays his crew good money to sit around doing nothing — I mean he pays for their time. They spend it lapping up liquor. Kane buys out Ira's half-interest in a mine he's always laughed at, and then Ben Brush —"

"You ain't gettin' set to tell me Brush is working for Kane, are you?"

"What makes you think he isn't? Why else would Ben Brush be trying to get you killed off?"

"But you just said he wasn't — you said it was ridic'lous! Hell's hinges, Taisy! Everybody knows Curly Bill got Brush that star-packin' job."

"I don't care," Taisy cried. "If he thought he'd be better off working for Kane — if Kane offered him more money —"

"But Kane *despises* Ben Brush! He's been workin' tooth an' nail to get Brush run out of town!"

"I notice he's still around," Taisy sniffed. "If you should happen to ask me, I think Kane's talk about running Brush out of town is just a dust he's throwing up to hide his real intentions."

"And what do you suppose his real intentions are?" the colonel sputtered, eyeing Taisy with the look a lot of other gents have worn after finding themselves hogtied in the intricacies of arguing with a woman. "You're talkin' plumb foolish, girl — plumb foolish. Brush ain't workin' for Kane and never will be. In the first place Kane wouldn't have him, an' Brush

90

wouldn't dast cross Curly Bill. Gosh a'mighty! Just because a man lets on he'd like to travel double with you —" The colonel shook his head like women were beyond him. "Just what do you figure Mister Kane is up to?"

"I think he's after your mine!" Taisy said.

The colonel threw up his hands. "Lord deliver us!" He snatched up his hat.

Taisy's shoulders stiffened. "Dad — please! Don't go up to the mine this evening."

"I'm not goin' to the mine," he said testily. "I'm —"

"Can't you stay and help me a little? You know cook's —"

"I can't help that."

"But what if Brush —"

"Can't help that, either! I'm not goin' to let a young feller I'm beholden to rot in no dadburned jail if I can help it."

"But you can't help it, Dad. Brush won't —"

"Brush'll listen to Comstock Kane, by godfreys, or we'll dang well know the reason why! Comstock swings a lot of weight in this town. I'm goin' to fetch him down here an' —"

"Oh, well," Taisy smiled, trying hard to

dissemble, "if it will make you feel better to go through the motions. . . . But you're not going alone — now don't argue! You're not going out on that street by yourself!"

Her father glared. "A fine sight I'll make tied onto your apronstrings!"

He scowled and snorted.

Taisy squared her shoulders and caught up her bonnet. She took his arm firmly. "I'm ready," she said.

If she sounded a little grim it was because of her feelings. She didn't want to do this. She didn't want at all to go out on the street. She didn't want to hurt her father's pride and dignity and she certainly had no desire to see Comstock Kane. But there was a lot of things you had to do in this world that were not compatible with personal inclination.

She was going just in case her Dad was right about Brush. She was going in the hope that, seeing her with him, Brush would pass up for the moment any further plans he'd made.

The colonel, still glaring and spluttering of apronstrings, stumped down the steps like a cat with its paws wet. Taisy said, "If you've got to be quixotic I shall be foolish with you — and it *is* foolish. You know it is! That gun fighter won't be cooped up in jail. He's probably in some bar carousing with the rest of them."

They set off for Kane's residence enveloped by the chill silence of the colonel's affronted dignity.

9

A VOICE IN THE NIGHT

Brand, listening to the marshal's ominous words, knew a sudden desperation. Once he let them get him locked away in the jail, he would have to stay there till they felt like releasing him and, from present indications, that would be a long time. He had no more desire to be in jail than the next man, yet what could he do with that gun pointing at him? He didn't believe Brush had been boasting when he'd mentioned shooting prisoners who'd been trying to escape. For Whit to attempt anything under the circumstances would be playing right into the marshal's hands.

Nevertheless, Whit Brand considered it. He was an outdoor man with all an outdoor man's aversion to cramped quarters. Once they got him locked in he might never get out. It might even be Brush's secret plan, once they got him in jail, to stir up a mob to the point of violence — a mob that would demand that the marshal surrender him. Such things happened. They might happen to him.

Obviously the marshal was embarrassed by Whit's presence. There wasn't any doubt in Whit's cogitating mind but that the smooth-talking Brush would be glad to see the last of a man whose tongue, if allowed free rein, might prove disastrous to his plans as well as downright dangerous. Brush was up to something crooked.

"Come on," the marshal said impatiently. "Left foot up an' right foot down! Boost him in there, Corrado!"

Corrado still retained his grip on Whit's twisted arm. Whit was between Corrado and the closed door to the cell block and the Mexican was between Whit and Brush's pistol. It was now or never.

Setting himself, throwing caution to the winds, Whit stamped his left bootheel on Corrado's nearest instep. Corrado let out a howl. Whit yanked his arm free. Still crowding the off-balance Mexican, Whit whirled and flung the man straight at the marshal. It was lightning-fast work and caught the marshal by surprise. Trying to avoid the Mexican's hurtling shape, Brush tripped and staggered and Whit was instantly on him as Corrado crashed into the desk and went down.

But Brush was stronger than he looked and, though taken by surprise, he kept his head and fought savagely to retain his hold on the pistol Whit was after. Whit had clamped a fierce grip on the marshal's wrist and was trying every trick he knew to force Ben Brush to let go of the weapon.

Backward and forward they swayed, locked and panting. Twisting, straining, stamping this way and that as they staggered round the room. One of the chairs smashed beneath their onslaught. Whit could see Corrado clawing up from the floor and kicked the man down again as they went rocking past him.

They crashed into a door, fought past it, Brush trying to hammer Whit's head against the wall. They were too well matched, Whit saw with despair. Tough Ben Brush was as strong as Whit was and neither one of them could seem to gain any advantage that was not immediately offset by some quick shift of the other. If the struggle were continued there could be but one end to it. Corrado would come to the marshal's aid.

And then the break came.

Brush, trying to whirl Whit into a wall

again, staggered into the bucket and lost his balance. He flung an arm round Whit's neck and pulled Whit with him. His weight dragged them both to the floor.

The pistol spun out of the marshal's hand and Corrado, bloody-faced, crawling toward them, grabbed it.

Whit was on top. He let go of Brush's wrist and slugged for his jaw. But the marshal twisted, got his head away. The blow rolled off his hunched up shoulder and he brought up a knee that jarred all Whit's breath out. Corrado crashed the barrel of Brush's gun on Whit's head.

Whit woke up in a cell, on the floor, where they'd thrown him. Every bone in his body ached with dull misery and his head felt like a granite cliff had hit it.

He pulled himself onto the cot and cursed.

He guessed he'd have plenty of time to think now.

The jail wasn't new — at least the building wasn't. Built of heavy adobe, it was probably an old ranch house, remodeled when Galeyville commenced to be a town and the need for a jail became increasingly apparent. The walls were better than two feet thick and the bars at the window were sunk deep into it. Not an impossible place to break out of, perhaps, but a place Whit would not be leaving in a hurry.

Not without help.

If he'd had a knife — but he hadn't. The marshal had taken everything from his pockets, even including his change. There was nothing whatever Whit could dig at that wall with, unless. . . .

He wondered with a scowl if a bootheel could do it. It might, he decided, if a man had time enough. With patience and a considerable outlay of energy a man might, in time, wear through to those bars. But it would take more time than Whit would ever have available. They were bound to come around, if only at mealtimes. Long before he could hope to get loose Brush or Corrado would discover what he was up to. If he fooled with that adobe there'd be no way to hide it — they might even hear him working. He could sure hear them plainly enough, muttering yonder.

He sat back on the cot and scowled bitterly at the door bars. The cot was piled with filthy blankets and smelled to high heaven. Also, it was bolted to the floor.

He got up and limped around.

The one window looked out upon a trash-littered alley. Like enough Brush would be setting out yonder with a sawed-off shotgun.

He wasn't, but he was going to. He came clumping his boots down to Whit's door and looked in at him. "I'll be settin' out there with a shotgun," he said, "an' the first yap out of you I'll come back here an' use it. Dead prisoners don't give me no trouble."

He went off with a scowl and Whit sighed resignedly.

The only people in this town who might conceivably be interested at all in Whit were Brush, Curly Bill and old man Wainright. He could look for no help from the first pair and the colonel seemed a pretty frail reed to lean on. Whatever he might feel disposed to do, it was a cinch that redhead would be sure to stop it. She would never let the colonel become further embroiled over any "cheap drifting gun-slick."

He wondered what could have turned her against him. Didn't seem like a girl as sweet-looking as she was would be getting such a down on a man over nothing. Worry for her Dad didn't call for such suspicion; there was bound to be more behind it than that. Seeing him talking with Bill must explain part of it, but that didn't satisfy Whit too well, either. She would have to hate Bill almighty bad to be venting her feelings on a stranger that way, and he could think of no reason for her hating Bill that much. Bill's business methods wouldn't seem to account for it. She was a heap too riled, too personal about it.

Whit shrugged, put the matter away with a grimace. There were a lot more urgent things to be considered than the foibles and fancies of a freckle-faced filly.

He wondered why Brush would want to gun down her father.

Had Brush killed Mell Snyder and grabbed the Planchas payroll? If he had, whereabouts could he have hidden the money? Whit had been all over the scene of that holdup; he would have sworn on any number of bibles that no strongbox had been buried within a mile of that place — and if it hadn't been buried, what the devil had become of it?

By the look of that ground there could not have been any other man in the holdup besides the dead Snyder. There wasn't enough horse sign for Mell to have had any extra horse with him. Since Mell had not got away, nor Mell's horse either, what in hell's hinges had become of that strong-box?

That was the burning question, Whit thought. The road had skirted some cliffs a couple of miles farther on. The box could have been heaved over them, but how had the unknown killer of Snyder ever gotten the box that far in the first place without leaving sign?

The payroll had probably been made up entirely of coin. Hard rock men didn't like folding money. So before it went into the strong-box at all, it had probably been sacked. A man on a horse would find it sort of inconvenient to lug off one of those express company boxes; they were cumbersome affairs and plenty heavy in themselves. But sacked stuff was prime for a man on a horse; like enough that was how the payroll had vanished. But what had become of the strong-box then? It might be down in that gulch, and it probably was, but Whit couldn't see how the devil it had got there from where Mell Snyder had held up the stage.

He shook his head, scowling, tramped a couple of turns around the confines of his cell. And he still couldn't see it.

There hadn't been a track of man or horse leaving the place where Mell had been shot down. Nothing but the tracks of Mell's own horse approached it — except the stage, of course, and the stagecoach horses. And no one else had since used the road unless Whit's eyes had suddenly lost all their cunning.

His mind returned to Brush.

He wondered what kind of a game Brush was playing. He wondered at the marshal's brashness in daring to heckle Curly Bill as he had. And more than anything else, Whit wondered why the owl-hoot boss, if as tough as reputed, had stood there and taken it.

He wondered about a whole passle of things but he couldn't find many believable answers.

He thought about Curly Bill for a bit. Curly Bill Graham was held to be some pumpkins in matters pertaining to guts and daring and the dexterous handling of long-barreled pistols. Curly Bill had vision and enterprise; he was no cheap crook, no fly-by-night robber. He was one of the boldest outlaws of his time and age; danger was his special dish and no kind of hardship had ever given him pause save the unromantic hardship of honest toil. His colorful exploits and tempestuous antics had furnished much material for after-supper yarns round the campfires of the cow camps, but astonishing and apocryphal as these deeds were, Curly Bill had his eyes on the main chance always. His crimes were commissioned on a business basis; he undertook nothing for effect or glory. He was quick and cunning and dangerous as a rattlesnake at skin-shedding time, for all his jovial manner.

Yet Ben Brush had told him off like a range bum.

Was Curly Bill scared of the shad-bellied marshal? He had not looked scared. Then why hadn't he loosed his wolf on Brush? Why had he stayed his hand when Brush had thrown those saturnine taunts in his teeth?

The voices out front quit after a while and Whit heard the slam of the outside door. He guessed they were off to lap up their suppers and gloomily wondered if they'd think to fetch him some.

This might be a pretty good time, he thought, to see what if anything he could do about getting himself out of that place. Those window bars looked to be the best bet and he was just starting toward them when the clomp of boots on the spur-scratched floor told him one of the pair was still in Brush's office.

He wondered which had gone, the boss or the boot-licker — not that it was likely

103

to make his cell any softer or this continued confinement any less irksome whichever had departed. There wasn't much else he could do but wonder.

Nevertheless, after a while, he went over and looked out. It was getting dark outside. Sunset tinted the slopes east of town, down there off beyond the edge of the mesa, and there was a breeze springing up, blowing out of the canyon, strong with the scent of flowering greasewood and palo verde. It sure made him ache to get out of there. It was the time of day Whit had always liked best, and he watched the shadows piling up like haze where the tangles of brush grew out of the hollows, turning the yonder rims blue and then purple.

It was getting dark fast, yet he could still plainly see the black shape of a wagon where someone had left it across the mouth of the alley. That reminded him of one of the men he'd once lived with after he had lost his folks in the massacre, the gent who had him before Ark Tummer had raked him in with the rest of the pot he had won on pat aces that night at Jade Crawfin's.

That seemed a long ways back to Whit now.

His thoughts veered to the girl whose picture he had carried, to Taisy Wainright, the sorrel-topped spitfire whose likeness had drawn him there like a magnet; and he frowned, thinking glumly of the welcome she had given him. Of course she didn't know it was her picture which had fetched him — and wild horses wouldn't get him to admit it to her now. Or to anyone else again, by godfreys! He could see the scorn curling back her red lips. She was sure plumb hostile. And considerable on the practical side. You'd never take her in with any wooden nutmegs! The colonel might wear the pants in his family, but Whit would have bet she did the bossing.

If he ever got out of that dadburned jail. . . .

Whit snorted, disgusted, and planked himself down on the pine-slat cot again, shoving the blankets off on the floor. He reckoned his luck had run out, and no kidding. No telling what that guy, Brush would do — no telling what Curly Bill would do, either. Bill would probably be nursing that kick in the chest.

Whit felt like a duck between the pan and the fire. If he got out of jail Curly Bill would be after him. If he didn't get out. . . .

Whit's scowl grew blacker, his look more dour, as he paced the narrow confines of his cell. He hadn't eaten all day and was hungry enough to gnaw the hide off a saddle. Misery ached in every bone, but he was too choused around by his thoughts to relax long. He was filled with a restless energy, with a tremendous urge to get out of that place. Sight of those gleaming bars acted on him like the flick of a red rag acts on a bull. He caught the bars of the window in a strangling grip. They were cold as dead snakes, as unaffected. He dropped them, shuddering. Then anger rushed through him and he wrapped his hands around them again, shook at them, pushed them, tugging, till he was drenched with sweat, but they were too well set, they did not give in the least; and it was their refusal to yield to his temper that showed him finally how irrevocably, how completely, he was under Brush's thumb.

It was a hateful thought. In a way it was terrifying. To admit it was to own he was not his own master.

He wasn't. Not in there. He was a bug in a bottle.

A light flared up in the front office.

Whit shook the bars of his door, swearing softly, watching the glimmer of that glow steal past, pulling dull gleams from the bars around him, driving their monstrous shadows along the walls, glinting off the barred doors just across the dark passage.

He wondered what old man Wainright was doing. The girl, he reckoned, would be getting supper — he could almost smell the appetizing aromas curling up with the steam from the bubbling lids of the pots.

He cursed his too active mind for its fancies. Thought of food made him hungry as a horse. Used to being his own boss and doing what he felt like when the notion struck him, this present inactivity was maddening.

He grabbed hold of the cell door bars again and glared toward the glow of the lamplit office. Maybe he would find some way to get out yet.

Yeah. Maybe.

Chances didn't grow on the bushes round there. But just the toehold of a chance was all he would ask for. Just the ghost of a chance — any part of one! Just give him one thing that he could get his teeth hooked in!

As sometimes happens, Brand's prayer was answered.

The answer came in the form of a hardly

heard whisper. It drifted in through the bars of one high window.

"Brand!" the voice pleaded. "Oh, Brand — are you in there?"

10

THE GREEK
BEARING GIFTS

Taisy! Brand thought, bouncing up off his cot. *Taisy Wainright had come with some plan to free him!*

Then he stopped, suddenly stiffening, and looked toward the bars.

That was foolish — plumb crazy. That was wishful thinking. Taisy Wainright would never come there to free him. She had made it right plain she didn't think he needed freeing.

Very carefully, still thinking, Whit moved toward the window. Whispers were deceptive. It was not at all likely to be Taisy out there — it wasn't even likely that the whisperer was a girl, though he was willing to believe that it was intended he think so.

He came beneath the window but he did not at once straighten. That was probably what they wanted, that he look out there. Peer right out into the face of a bullet!

He was not that dumb.

He hoisted his hat on the end of a finger and raised it enough to show the crown in the opening. When still nothing happened he kept the hat held there and, after a bit, the whisper was repeated. "Is that you, Brand?" It sounded urgent, excited.

Whit rose on his boot toes and peered through the bars.

He was not too surprised to see the face of Corrado. It was pretty dark out there but not too dark for him to recognize the man. He looked into the fellow's foxy face, disgusted.

"What brings you here?" he growled, glowering down at him. " 'F you had a buzzard's politeness you'd wait till I'm dead —"

"*Sangre de Cristo!*" Corrado's scared whisper squeaked like a gate hinge. "*Maldito!*" he swore. "Keep down the voice — you weesh for tell the whole town?"

"If I'm goin' t' get killed I want folks to know it," Whit grumbled, and the whites of the Mexican's eyes glowed wildly. He looked like a rat about to scuttle away again.

"All right," Whit said, speaking more

softly, "what's up? Who you reppin' for, Brush or William?"

"Weelyum?"

"Curly Bill," Whit growled, losing his patience. "What you up to out there? Tryin' to stick a knife in me?"

Corrado stared up at Whit. He peered at him nervously. "You like for stay een these place? Ees comfortable — no? All the time eat, sleep —"

"Never mind the palaver. Aimin' to spring me?"

Corrado flung a quick look through the round-about shadows. "Can do," he said, nodding vigorously, looking up at Whit and showing his teeth.

"What's the catch?" Whit said. "What you stallin' around for?"

"You want to get out?"

"If I want to get out I'll do it without no help from you."

Corrado's grin grew wider. "I'm not theenk so."

"All right. What's the catch? What you bargainin' for?"

"Ees no bargain. Only the fool eenspec' the geeft horse' teet'. Smart hombre, she's jomp right away een the saddle — vamoose pronto!"

Whit thought fast. This might be a trap,

probably was, but trap or no trap, the man was offering him a chance and Whit was in no shape to be playing Lord Choosy.

It was entirely in the cards that Corrado and the marshal had rigged this deal up as a means of avoiding later embarrassment. It might be on the square, but Whit did not believe this. Brush would be wanting him dead or plumb out of the country; he could not afford to have Whit loose and talking. If he got killed outside, obviously bent on escape, it would look a lot better for the marshal of Galeyville than for anything to happen while Whit still was in jail. It might take some explaining were Whit's blood to be found splattered over the floorboards.

That was probably the answer.

There would not be so many questions to answer if Whit were shot running down that alley. Brush was out to get old man Wainright — he'd already made one try. He probably wanted to make sure, before he started another, that Brand wasn't going to be around to squawk. Of course the girl still might talk, but Brush wouldn't care what a girl said.

Whit considered these things and a number of others, but he knew mighty well that if Brush wanted him dead there were plenty of ways a smart marshal could fix it — and there was still Curly Bill to consider.

If Bill really figured Whit had got that payroll, remaining locked in that jail was the last thing Whit wanted. So when the Mexican said again, more sharply, "You no want for get out of these place?" Whit put conjecture aside and nodded.

Corrado's dark and lean-carved face twisted round and looked up at him. " 'Sta bueno," he said, smacking his lips in a grin. "I get you out you be the scarce pronto. No 'ang aroun' or they poot you to bed weeth the peek an' the shovel."

Whit grunted, impatient. "Never mind all that. How you figurin' to work it?"

For answer the Mexican, bracing himself, ducked down out of sight and came up slowly, straining. He had in his hands the hooked end of a lumber chain. This he slipped cautiously through the barred window. Whit didn't ask what to do with it; tendering it an even greater care than Corrado had shown, he wove it slowly through the bars as, link by link, the mustached deputy handed him up more and more of the chain.

It was sweaty work and hard on the nerves, coupled as it was with the definite knowledge that one scrape of that chain against the cold bars would bring Brush running. When at last they had got it fastened securely, the derby-hatted Corrado stepped back a little and pointed a hand toward the mouth of the alley.

"You see heem? Those wagon? *A-a-ai-hé!* Fine and dandy! Pretty soon now — w'en she's feenish the sopper — these driver she's hook on the terms, *los caballos,* an' crack the wheep for the mines. You savvy the burro? Other end these chain she's wrap aroun' axle. W'en weendow fly out you fly weeth heem."

"You can say that again," Whit muttered. He wondered where in this catch-rigged deal he would find the joker. Bound to be a trick in the business somewhere. Corrado wasn't helping him out of love. He wasn't crossing Ben Brush up for nothing. He probably wasn't crossing up Brush at all — but time would tell.

Brand had a hunch this hand was from a deck stacked by malice, but there was no sense in hunting up stones to turn over. The play offered him a chance and that was all he asked for. First things first was an old cowboy axiom, and the first thing for Whit was to get himself out of there.

"What about my guns?"

Corrado shook his lean-carved face. "These gons, she are lock' in the marshal's desk — I'm no got the key."

"You got a horse for me, ain't you?"

The swarthy deputy sighed. His eyes touched Whit's keenly and then rolled away again. "Ees not possible, *señor.* The marshall 'ave poot *los caballos* een stable."

"Oh, well," Whit shrugged. *"No le hace."*

Corrado nodded. A moment later, after throwing quick glances up and down the alley, crouching low, he ducked off into the shadows. He slipped away through the trash with no more noise than a vinegarroon.

Whit stood there a long while, thinking.

11

A CAT LICKS HIS CHOPS

Brand had hardly turned away from the window when an increase of light suddenly swept down the corridor, throwing gleams off the bars and dancing black shadows along the white walls. He could hear boots clomping toward his cell and he stood there, frozen, while a thousand thoughts flew through his head and his heart set up a tom-tom beating.

Was this the test? Was Corrado's trap about to be sprung?

But no, Whit thought. Common sense assured him such an idea was loco. He was still in his cell. They could have killed him there without all that bother.

He remembered the chain and his heart stood still. It would show at the window! Had it been discovered? Had the freighter stumbled onto it and gone to the marshal?

But if he had, the marshal wouldn't be

coming alone. No, it wasn't that which was fetching Brush back there.

Maybe Brush didn't know about this deal after all.

But that chain —

Whit sweated. His stomach rose up and shoved at his teeth as he thought of that heavy chain around the bars that could be seen the minute Brush looked toward the window.

If Brush spotted that chain. . . .

Whit choked an oath and stood up nervously. He straightened tensely, eyes narrowed toward the sound of the approaching boot clomps. If he sat on his cot, would that keep Brush's eyes away from the window? If he stood by the door, would his shadow hide it? Would his body conceal it if he stood by the window?

Be a natural thing for Brush to look around. Wouldn't the window be the first place he'd look? Wouldn't he be suspicious if. . . .

While Whit stood sweating in the grip of indecision, his chance was lost. Brush and his lamp suddenly loomed at the door.

"Corrado," Brush said, "is feedin' his face. When he gets back you an' me will be goin'. Maybe you're thinkin' that's when you'll git loose — maybe you're thinkin'

Curly Bill will try somethin'. Jest wanted to remind you I'll be fetchin' a shotgun. I'd admire to see you try to get loose."

He grinned, thin and cold.

"You might make it at that," he said, and laughed in the silent way of an Indian. He swung bony shoulders and tramped back to his office.

Whit's mouth was dry as a cotton rag. He felt his knees start to shake and wabble. He sank down on the bunk and sleeved his face.

Brush hadn't once glanced toward the window.

Whit pulled a fresh breath deep inside himself. He was fetching an arm up to wipe sweat again when his hopes went into a million pieces.

The light had stopped. It was coming back. It was coming with the harsh sound of boots on the floorboards.

It was he, all right. Ben Brush, in person.

He strode on past Whit's door with the lamp. He went to the back wall, two cells away, reached up and set the lamp in a bracket.

Whit came out of his trance with a shudder. One quick stride took him over to the window; he could not expect Brush to miss it twice. He caught hold of the bars and stood there motionless. Tensely he stood there staring between them with his ears stretched wide to catch Brush's movements. His eyes dug into the outside shadows, made blacker by the lamp's yellow light. He prayed that his body might hide the chain, that Brush would not call him away from the window. He stood there stiff as frozen wax and waited for Brush to stop at the doorway.

He could tell by the sound Brush had turned and was coming. Each step he took brought doom's dread nearer. Whit's heart banged against his ribs with the foreknowledge of discovery and the marshal's approach was the longest thing ever engraved in his memory.

He could scarcely breathe.

He could feel the beat of his heart in his throat, in the strangle grip of his hands on the bars, even the bars themselves seeming to pulse with the rhythm of it. Each fall of the marshal's feet was like the feel of a nail being sunk in his coffin.

Whit strained his ears.

He heard Brush's clomping boots suddenly stop.

"Any time you're ready, just go right ahead."

Whit braced himself for the bite of lead,

to the feel of it ripping his body apart, to the deafening crash of it downing his cries.

But no gun barked.

"Just hop through them bars if you want t' meet Peter," said Brush's taunting voice, and his boots moved on, going up the corridor into his office.

Whit was too unnerved to even so much as swallow. He strangled the bars with his hands and shuddered. He clung to the bars with his sweaty fingers and tried to whip his thoughts into some order. It didn't seem possible Brush could have missed the chain twice. It didn't seem credible that Ben Brush could twice have looked into his cell and then have gone back to his office unknowing.

Yet that was apparently what Brush had done.

But had he?

No, Whit thought. The marshal knew.

He remembered the swell of Brush's sun-blackened cheeks, his smugness, his cat-sly stare. The man was playing with him — that was the answer! Brush was tickling himself by keeping Whit guessing. He was getting a cat's malicious pleasure out of letting Whit think he was getting away with it.

Let Brush play his games, let him have

his belly laughs. Let him have anything he wanted just so he didn't uncouple that chain from the wagon. . . .

A sudden thought crossed Whit's mind and left him scowling. What assurance did he have they'd ever hitched it to the wagon!

He went stiff again, listening.

Someone had just stepped off the board walk that went past the front of the jail to the alley. The man had there been joined by another; Whit could hear the brief mutter of arguing voices. He could hear footsteps going into the building next door, growing muted. Whit, pressing his face close against the bars, could make out the ramshackle lines of the place, could see the long sweep of the whoppy-jawed roof where it climbed up the sky and blacked out the bright stars; and, still staring, he made a discovery.

The place was a barn!

That astonished him hugely. He was surprised he had not sensed it sooner. Its nearest wall was not over twenty-five feet from the window. He heard horse sounds now, a muffled stomping and snorting. It was the driver, he guessed, gone to fetch out his teams and hook onto the wagon.

He could hear the men grumbling and

bickering. Then a door squeaked open and a guy with a lantern came bowlegging out and took up a stand by the front of the wagon, and a second man came with two jumpy broncs and swearingly backed the pair into their places.

Whit saw this one look at the other guy, glowering. "Who the hell ever called *you* a ornyment? Thet light ain't goin' to fly off ef you leave it! Set it down, by cripes, n' latch onto thet harness or you kin damn well fetch out the rest yourself!"

There was something about that bowlegged gent that scratched uncomfortably at the gates of Whit's memory. He could not immediately think what it was until, as the man bent over to put down his lantern, Whit got a look at his face and knew. Small wonder he had thought the guy looked familiar! The man was older now with a face marked by the ravages of whisky but Whit, gone tense, had no trouble in remembering him. That bowlegged buck was Arkansaw Tummer — the same Ark Tummer that had raked Whit in with a couple of aces during the game of stud at Jade Crawfin's that night — the same pie-eyed stinker!

Whit abandoned all plans for crawling that wagon. He would as soon have hooked a ride with the devil as with Tummer. It wasn't that he was scared of the man; he just didn't want any truck with him.

For a moment he was half tempted to undo the chain. He even went so far as to stretch a hand toward it; but with his hand upon it better judgment prevailed. There was no sense rotting in that jail to spite Tummer. Besides, by himself Whit would be bound to make considerable noise if he tried to throw off that chain from its fastenings. Better leave it right there where it was. There was always the chance he might be wrong about Brush; Brush might have no knowledge of that chain and the plot Corrado had hatched to free Whit. Better to let matters take their unhampered course and do what had to be done when he had to.

Whit watched them bring out the rest of the horses. When all five teams had been hitched to the wagon he saw Tummer start off on a tour of inspection. The man's legs weren't too steady but he still had them under him and Whit waited, scarcely breathing, in a sudden cold sweat lest the man discover the telltale chain.

But Whit needn't have worried. Tummer wasn't looking over his outfit; he was going through the motions out of habit more than anything. His mind was too befogged with the fumes of his drinking to be anything like remotely critical. He was too fool drunk to give a whoop about anything, and the second time he fell he gave up even the pretense. Whit watched him stumble back and climb into the wagon. As he stepped from the wheel he missed his footing and disappeared suddenly. Whit could hear his blurred oath from the depths of the wagon.

Whit's lips curled.

The man holding the horses now hurled his voice as he frantically fought to keep the lead team from bolting. Those half broke broncs were plain hell in the harness. "By godfreys," the man snarled. "Damned ef I'd hev such — *what the bloody hell are you doin'?*"

"I can't find m' whip!"

"Why, you whey-bellied idjit, it's right in yore hand!"

There was a sudden commotion out front in the office. If Whit had entertained doubts about the marshal's attitude he couldn't, in reason, do so any longer. Brush's boots were hurrying toward him. He wasn't wasting any time — he knew what his prisoner was up to. Like Tummer, pretending to look over his wagon, Brush had gone through the motions of a man being hoodwinked, but he hadn't been fooled for a minute. He had wanted Whit Brand to get out of there; all the time he'd been planning on this very wind-up. He wanted to kill Whit in the act of escaping!

12

THE JOKER IN THE DECK

Dread, wildly mixed with a white-hot anger, began pounding in Whit's arteries as he heard Brush coming. Much as he would have liked to settle the score with Ben Brush, it was one of those pleasures he would have to forego. He hadn't the time — he dared not wait for anything. Brush didn't have to get near him; with that sawed-off Greener he could kill Whit through the bars. When that window went out Whit would have to go with it. Brush was primed now to shoot whether Whit stayed or not.

All the horses were acting up now. The man couldn't begin to hold them. With a curse he let go and sprang aside. The man in the wagon bed swung his whip and the half broke broncs lunged into their collars.

Whit could feel his knees shaking as he caught at the bars. He braced both feet against the wall and tugged. He could

126

more easily have torn the moon from its orbit. The sound of Brush's boots in that ominous silence clouted toward him like thunder and then, with a grinding crunch and a clatter, the huge wagon lurched forward. There was a raucous clanging screech of metal as the rust-covered chain shifted hold on the bars.

One thought pounded through the growing terror in Whit's mind. The screech of that chain grinding over the bars still rang in his ears and the window wall still stood in its place, brick on brick and unshaken, yet Whit had that moment of coherent thought. Not even the bang of Brush's boots in the corridor could shake that one clear thought from his head. Corrado might have his own good reasons for hooking that chain to the bars of that window, but it was a heap more likely Ben Brush was behind it and, if this were so, for Whit to follow instructions would be practically the same as committing suicide.

Whit had got that far in his thinking when the window went out in a great cloud of dust, taking bars and casing and great chunks of adobe. But instead of diving after it as Corrado had advised him, Whit flung himself face down on the floor; and at that precise moment Brush's shotgun roared. He let go with both barrels and lead screamed over Whit's head like hail.

Then Whit was up, like a flash, diving after it.

Rage swelled in his throat as he lit on a shoulder and desperately rolled to get out of Brush's sight. The murderous devils! They had framed him, all right; they had planned the whole thing that they might kill him with safety! They were well within the letter of the law trying to kill an escaping prisoner, and only pure luck had saved Whit so far — only that last minute hunch had protected him.

And he wasn't clear yet — he wasn't clear by a jugful! Brush would be after him as quick as he could get that cell door open. Whit could hear him cursing as he jangled his keys; and then some fellow sprang into the alley mouth and cut loose with his hardware like hell wouldn't hold him. Whit could see his crouched shape between the bursts of his firing; he could hear the man's slugs slamming into the trash.

Not even the darkness could save Whit long, and he sprang to his feet, his heart pounding wildly.

There wasn't but one place left he could

go, and he ran for it — ran with every ounce of strength he could muster. Straight toward the back, toward the end of the alley. Doubled over and panting, he slammed his boots toward it. It was all he could do, the only choice left him. If the back end of this alley was blocked he was done for.

When Curly Bill Graham quit the marshal's office, he was about as mad as he ever had been. His great chest seethed with the tumult inside him. Never before in his life had he taken such a blistering. He was so furiously mad he crashed straight into a man without seeing him.

But the guy kept his balance and gave Bill a grin. They were old friends, those two, for the man was John Ringo, one of Curly Bill's sidekicks, the man some folks said was the brains of Bill's outfit. His teeth showed in a saturnine grin. He said, "What the hell is eatin' you, Curly?"

The rustler boss glared. It made him mad all over. He loosed a flood of language that would have blistered the varnish on the side of a coffin. "That blankety-blink-blank-blunk-in' Brush! I'm agoin' t' plant that feller ef it's the last thing I do!"

John Ringo was a man folks looked at twice. He had a lanky shape built high above his corns and a back that was straight as a gun barrel. His eyes were black and set deep in dark hollows and he bore the same relation to Bill as cadaverous Doc Holliday bore to Wyatt Earp; he was a Curly Bill man and everyone knew it. He understood Bill's ways and would straight out tell you Bill never forgave an injury or forgot a friend.

He looked at Bill sharply now and quit his grinning. When Bill talked like that it was high time someone had better watch out. "We better drift over to Babcock's," he said.

"Just a minute," Bill growled, staring down toward the Lone Star. "Where do you reckon them two is off to?"

Ringo, following his glance, merely shrugged. He was not a heap interested in the Wainrights himself, though he knew Bill was. "Looks to me like they might be headin' for Kane's."

"Yeah," Bill glowered. "Looks that way t' me, too. I don't like it," he said. "I've done put my brand on that gel, by godfreys, an' I ain't allowin' — The less she sees of that Kane," he snarled, "the better I'll like it! We had plenty good sleddin' till that fancy

130

pants come here. I got t' do somethin' about that feller, John. He's as big a Paul Pry as that damn Wyatt Earp!"

"You mean Kane?" Ringo said.

"I mean Kane." Curly Bill stared after the pair mighty dark like. "I think it's Kane that's been tamperin' with that tinplated Brush. When I give him that star he was jest plain coyote; now he sets up an' yaps like a wolf."

Ringo nodded, and then apparently thought of something else. "You think he's tamperin' with them payrolls?"

Bill stared, the whites of his eyes showing. "How could he? By cripes, he was right here in town about the time Mell Snyder was gettin' rubbed out — a man can't be two places at once. Leastways, not no man that I ever knowed. An' there wasn't no passengers on that stage — there wasn't nothin' on it but the driver an' the guard, an' them two ore sacks of specimens Kane got."

Ringo's eyes showed the darkness of his thoughts. He looked at Bill slanchways.

"Oh, they was specimens, right enough," Curly Bill said. "I checked with the driver. He's handled enough t' know ore when he hefts it. It was some of that stuff Kane sent up t' the assayer's office."

Ringo nodded indifferently. He got out his tobacco sack and fashioned a cigarette. Curly Bill's glowering eyes observed the deftness of his fingers with a smoldering kind of quiet. His flushed face held the look of a prodded bull; there was the same savagery about him, the same urge toward violence. It was a mark of their relation that this burly boss of badmen seldom ever bothered to hide his feelings from John Ringo.

They were as far as the poles apart, those two, at least to outward seeming. Bill was burly, blustering, profane, a man of strong appetites, loud and gusty in his laughter. Ringo was a quiet man. He had an introspective, tragic look and was plainly born to better things than those with which he surrounded himself in that roaring camp on the wild frontier. He was Bill's right hand and, as such, he could usually be found in the thick of Bill's projects, prominent in Bill's forays, in his drinking and his gambling. Yet, even so, he was a man apart. Tall and lean and saturnine, he remained ever a man of mystery, though plenty of gents would tell you he'd come West to bury his past. If so, he had found, as had many another, that more than drink and distance were needed to blot out the things in a man's mind. He had moods of bitter melancholy and sometimes spoke of killing himself. By his occasional choice of unusual words he appeared to have been well educated, though mostly he took a perverse delight in carving up the king's English. He had fallen far but there was still about him a look and a manner that set him apart from the rest of Bill's men, no matter what lengths he went to be like them.

He was a man with wheels in his think-box.

He was a man whose word, once given, was kept. He treated all women with a courtly chivalry. He was known to have come from Texas, to have been mixed up in a sheep and cattle feud in which his only brother had been foully murdered, and his vengeance had called for a hasty departure. All over the West men had known John Ringo, a drifter who lived by his wits and his gambling, by the cold glinting speed of his ivory-butted pistols. He was a man handsomely known in his own right and had no need to bask in Bill's glory. He must have thrown in with Bill to take his mind off the specters that haunted it.

He was a man who stood for the old tradition, a man who believed in survival of the fittest. He was openly resentful when the Earps' puritanical influence finally made Bill decide to move out of Tombstone. He considered Bill's shift to Galeyville an outrage and for several weeks afterward had taken desperate measures to incite Tombstone residents into ridding themselves of the octopus that was, to use his own contemptuous description, turning their town into the facsimile of a women's sewing circle.

People looked for trouble every time John Ringo rode into the town. No one doubted he was spoiling for a fight. He took no trouble to hide his opinions and openly flaunted his ivory-butted pistols in the faces of the Earps whenever he could find them, but the Earps steadfastly refused to take issue, and he had finally abandoned the place in disgust.

Some of that disgust was still reflected in his face as he shaped up his cigarette and stuck it in his mouth. He held a light to its end and regarded Bill dourly, and after a while said thoughtfully: "You think Ben's sold us out?"

"That's how the cards read t' me," Bill growled, and in a lowered voice went over the deal from the time Whit Brand had ridden in with Mell's body. "An' now Brush's talkin' of paw an' beller!"

John Ringo's saturnine eyes brightened. He loosened the pistols in their dark oily holsters. "That damn blackleg's gettin' plumb insolent," he said, and swung about, quick and catlike, starting toward Brush's office.

"Wait — hold on!" Bill growled, grabbing hold of him. "We can't afford no plays like that — we got to keep in mind what that son said. He wouldn't hev the guts to talk up to me that way without he had a pretty sure hole-card."

"Well," Ringo said, "he's a pretty tough cookie."

"He ain't that tough!" Bill swore again.

"What about this guy Brand?" John Ringo asked. "You think he jumped Snyder after Mell held the stage up?"

"Damn if I know. He had McLown's empty wallet right enough, I reckon. You think Mell tried t' pull a sandy on us? You reckon it was Mell that grabbed McLown's wallet?"

Ringo thought for a while, finally shook his head. "How would he have known about McLown's deal with Kane? You don't even know Brand had McLown's wallet — all you know is what Brush told you."

"Yeah." Bill scowled. His eyes glowered more blackly.

"If someone stole Ira's wallet and the money Kane paid him — if any," Ringo said, "it must of been some gent Mister Kane put up to it. Consider the facts. Ira might have talked, but he says he didn't. Says he never told a soul. All the rest of the bunch that was in Shotwell's store that night says the same. So the feller that grabbed it must have been tipped off by Kane himself. I never did like the guy." Ringo said with his lip curled. "Too glib with his jaw — gives off too much chin music."

"Mebbe Kane grabbed it himself," Bill growled, but Ringo shook his head. "Kane's too slick to make a play of that kind. He might of got it but I don't think he grabbed it. Why should he? Plenty of guys he could hire for such didos. That's a pretty tough crew he's got workin' that mine. If Kane's back of Brush —"

"Kane's back of him, all right." Curly Bill took the lid off his can of cusswords. "If that bastard has his way he's goin' t' run us outa here!"

"Mebbe," Ringo grinned, "we better pay Kane a visit."

It was Bill who shook his head that time. "We got t' play this careful. The guy's got too big in these diggin's now. If we tried any rough stuff an' it didn't come off we'd git run plumb outa these mountings. Only reason we been let alone this long is account of we ain't never bothered these local sports, these mine-ownin' dudes that calls theirselfs 'solid citizens.' You touch one of them, Galey or Kraftner or this Kane, an' you'll stir up —"

"They'll take a fling at it anyway sooner or later." Ringo frowned, his face darkly thoughtful. "I don't like the way folks been whisperin' round here. I can't never catch them at it but I know they're doin' it. Puts me in mind of the way it got at Charlston."

"So you've noticed that, hev you?" Bill's black eyes snapped. "I ort t' line 'em all up an' shoot 'em down like dawgs!"

He stamped around a couple of times and glared again toward the hash house. "By Gawd, I kin still make out t' add two an' two! If this guy thinks he's goin' t' put the skids under *me* —"

He broke off, looked at Ringo again, his eyes turned crafty. "It's goin' t' take some figgerin', but I got a little idear in my head."

"What you goin' to do about this two-by-four Brand?"

"That's what I'm gittin' at. There's a heap about that feller I don't rightly savvy . . . like about Mell Snyder an ' that stagecoach job. Like about McLown's wallet an' where Brush comes into it. What was Brand doin' with O'Dade's flea-bit gray? What was he doin' when Brush laid hold of him? What for did he jug him? There's a pile I don't know; but there's one thing I *do* know. Brand's the joker in this deck an' I figger t' use him."

Ringo stroked his jaw, considered Bill and nodded. "How?"

"You'll see," Bill said, cuffing dust off his chaps. "Look at that tie rail frontin' the Lone Star. That's O'Dade's horse. Drift over there an' git him. I'm goin' to make some medicine. I'm goin' to find out why Kane closed his Planchas mine up. I'm goin' t' find out why he bought into Wainright's Folly. This feller O'Dade is one of Kane's teamsters. I'm goin' t' look up O'Dade. . . . But right off now you git hold of that horse an' cache him out some place where we'll hev him handy just as quick's it gits dark. When you git that done, come over to Babcock's — I'll be in the back room. I'm goin' t' show you how we kin fix Kane's clock."

13

A MAN'S LUCK

Trapped in the gloom of that trash-choked alley, threatened on the left by Brush and his shotgun, blocked from the street by the man with the pistol, hemmed to the right by the barn's blank wall, Whit Brand knew the feeling of a wolf at bay.

The slap of those shots and their screaming lead, the whistle and clang of ricochets, roused in Whit a bitter frenzy of anger that rocked and shook him though he knew it impotent. He was filled with a consuming desire to get at them, to pay them back in kind, to rend and batter — to feel them squirm in his hands, to see their eyes bugging out, to hear them plead for mercy. He had an almost ungovernable impulse to disregard danger, to whirl and go after them, but he knew the futility of any such action. He must escape, and quickly.

Caution could not help him now. There was no place to hide where their slug wouldn't find him. With doubt before and death behind, unarmed, he had no choice but to run. They had nothing to fear; they would close in swiftly, eager for the kill.

Who lives by the gun — he thought, and cursed.

With black rage in his heart, bent double and weaving, he ran toward the black rear end of the alley.

A whole column of men raced past the ends of the buildings, the smell of their dust drifting into Whit's nostrils, the thunder of their steps stilling for the moment the sound of his flight through the tin cans and bottles. Men's boots hammered on the board walks out front, and the high-pitched avid-sounding call of their voices, but Whit ran on.

Twice he fell but got up again, snarling, and went lunging on. In that racketing bedlam of shouts and curses, of flying lead and pistol crashes, no one was listening. They had no need. They knew he was trapped. They knew they had him. This had been their plan, their intention from the first, from the very first word Corrado had whispered!

He heard a man's boots go pounding upstairs, the slam of a door. Then the guns took up an increased hammering and lead droned through the dark again, viciously whacking through unseen obstacles. The way it would whack through him if it found him.

Whit suddenly stopped and crouched tensely, listening. Why was Brush's shotgun staying so silent? What was holding him? Why wasn't he firing?

All the gun sounds suddenly quit, their clattering echoes falling away to whispers. No sounds of pursuit broke through that quiet — no calls, no questions, just a black wave of silence creeping through the alley. It was a smothering fog settling round him, like invisible fingers reaching for his windpipe.

What were they up to? What were they scheming?

They couldn't have lost him — or could they? Was there, after all, some place he might hide? Were they sneaking up to it, thinking he'd gone there? Was that the answer to the sudden silence? Or were they crouched there, waiting, guns lifted and ready, listening for a sound they could target their lead on?

Sweat was cold on Whit's cheeks and his heart was pounding. He tried to hold the pant of his breathing lest it give him away to these wolves in Law's clothing, to these blood-sucking weasels with kill-hungry guns.

Not till his pulse had slowed down a little did he dare to move at all, and then, slow and careful, he moved only his head, turning it cautiously, trying to probe the mealy darkness around him. He saw nothing at all but the bulk of the barn and, off to the left, the building housing the jail. There was nothing between them that showed or moved.

Whit was not fooled.

They were there, all right. They were out there some place. Somewhere in the gloom of that too quiet alley they were watching and waiting for Whit to betray himself. They hadn't gone and their very stillness showed they knew he was there, that sooner or later he would have to start moving.

They could wait. Whit couldn't.

Time was Whit's nemesis. The longer he stayed there the better their chances.

He wished he knew how close they were, and if those others he'd heard in the street had joined them. Brush and Corrado were probably the nearest. They'd not be far apart. The man from the street, the man with the pistol, had probably come up the alley behind Whit. That was probably

142

Corrado, coming back from his supper. Brush had only to step through that torn out window to be halfway up the alley's length. He must have done so long since.

The quiet had grown thick enough to cut by now. Through it Whit could hear a sudden upswing of voices and laughter, the stamping of feet and the clink of glasses, from Jack Dall's saloon three doors up the street.

He swung another quick look through the piled up shadows and silently cursed the thick gloom that concealed him, for it also concealed Ben Brush and Corrado, who knew the place much better than he. They would not be much impeded by darkness. He remembered how soundlessly Corrado had moved after fixing his chain to the bars of that window.

Whit's nerves were as tight as fiddle strings but he knew he could not remain there much longer. At any moment other men might join the search if they had not already.

Bending down, he put a cautious hand to the ground. He moved it a little and touched the smooth hard surface of a bottle. He closed his fingers around its neck. It was an unbroken bottle, an empty fifth.

He hefted it gently and paused, considering. There was a mighty good chance such experienced hands as Brush and the Mexican would not be deceived by the striking of an object against another. Still, they might be. If Whit tossed that bottle they could not be sure the resultant sound was not made by Whit's boots starting forward again. Should the bottle strike trash and roll a little, they would probably fire anyway. If he tossed it carefully they would not hear a thing until the bottle landed.

He had to do something. He decided to chance it. It would be suicide to move before discovering their whereabouts. Under cover of their firing he might get clear of them.

But he did not toss the bottle even then. First he bent down and felt around with his other hand, felt around till his fingers got hold of a can. Thus armed, he straightened.

He drew back both arms, throwing can and bottle simultaneously.

There was a thump and a rattle and, over by the barn, a six-shooter blossomed in a violent staccato, bursts of flame licking out from it wickedly, briefly showing vague portions of the shape behind it.

But Whit kept his place. All geared to

144

run, he stood there frozen, a strong sense of danger holding him rooted. Brush hadn't fired. Brush had been too smart to be taken in by Whit's trick, and until he knew Brush's whereabouts, Whit dared not move.

Corrado, reloading his pistol, was muttering.

He could hardly have felt more balked than Whit did. The failure of his ruse had left Whit panicky. What if Corrado should strike a light? It wasn't likely he would, but someone else might, one of those men crouching by the alley mouth.

Every moment Whit stayed there was lessening his chances. He swung half around, sorely tempted to bolt. Anything, he thought, would be better than waiting.

Remembrance of the sound of Corrado's pistol hurling its drumming lead at the bottle helped him to beat down that urge, to lick it.

A little wind pushing up through the darkness felt good to the sweat that was filming his cheekbones. A fierce resentment welled up inside him. Why was Brush so determined to kill him? It did not seem commensurate with what he had done. All he'd done, after all, had been to knock Brush down — to unsaddle Brush's dignity, perhaps to foil Brush's plans for a little while. But was that any reason for killing him? Even out here it seemed hard to believe that a man could be killed with no more compunction than was being exhibited by Brush and his Mexican.

One thing was certain. This was no game they were playing. Brush and Corrado were in deadly earnest. They were after his hide and, no matter what impulse hooked their fingers around triggers, he'd be just as dead if their slugs ever struck him.

He clenched his teeth and peered round through the shadows.

Then something turned his eyes suddenly narrow. He was remembering the picture, that picture of Taisy that had fetched him into this. It was back in Brush's office with the rest of his stuff. Though he didn't want to lose it, Whit was far from foolish enough to risk going back for it. It wasn't the picture he considered going back for, it was that eight hundred dollars Ben Brush had taken off him. And his hardware. With a gun in his fist. . . .

His face narrowed, Whit stared through the gloom toward that broken window. If he could get back inside . . . He didn't see any reason going back there would be a bit harder than going any other place — it might be easier. They wouldn't be expecting him to pull a stunt like that. They wouldn't be watching the jail any more. They'd be watching the one hole they'd left to entice him — the black rear end of this alley.

And if he could get back into the jail again, get his guns and his money, he could walk out the front and probably never be noticed.

The more he considered it the smarter it looked. Brush would feel like a fool if Whit got clear of him that way. It would take some doing for Brush to live that down. And the plan had the merit of looking a heap safer than any other thing Whit could do at the moment.

He felt around on the ground till he got hold of a tin can.

Crouched that way, carefully balanced on one hand and a knee, Whit heaved the can toward the curdled murk they'd been driving him into, those impenetrable shadows at the back of the alley.

The can struck with a resounding clatter that was instantly drowned in the pulsating roar of the Mexican's pistol. While Whit had stood thinking, Brush's derby-hatted helper had been inching forward until now, when he fired, he was nearly abreast of Whit ten feet away.

Whit waited no longer.

At the first blasting roar of that pistol Whit dived through the gloom toward that jagged black hole in the jailhouse wall. In less than six heartbeats he was clambering through it. The gun was still crashing when he dropped to the floor.

The lamp Brush had put in the hallway was out. Whit breathed a quick thanks for this small favor and felt for the door bars. The cell door was open. Whit went through it quickly, thinking Brush had been in no mood to waste time locking it after the jail's only prisoner had fled. He stepped into the corridor and went on up it and flipped the latch of the office door.

The office was dark and appeared to be empty. The growl of men's voices came from the street and Corrado's gun again blasted the blackness off toward the rear of the jailhouse alley.

Whit felt his way to the desk, and swore. Ben Brush had locked it.

Whit racked his mind for something that would open it but could think of nothing that would turn the trick. Nor could he remember there being anything in the office.

A good stout knife was what he needed. A case knife would do it.

He felt with his fingers along the edge of the desk where the roll-top fastened. He could move it a little. He felt through his pockets, but Brush had been thorough; he hadn't left so much as a cartwheel in them. Whit thought of his belt and whipped it off. If he could get the buckle wedged into that crack . . .

He could, and did. He put his weight on it.

The top whipped up with a sudden sharp snap.

Whit's hands were swift to feel inside it. He found his money where Brush had left it but his searching fingers couldn't locate his guns. He pocketed the money with an imprecation. McLown's wallet was there and probably the picture, but it was his guns Whit wanted right now, and badly.

He felt around again with no better luck.

It was too dark in there to see anything. It wouldn't be smart to light any matches, but if he'd had one then he would have scratched it pronto. A gun in his fist would help even the odds, and he'd really been counting on finding one in there. He tried the desk drawers but he couldn't budge any of them. He tried to think if there'd been other guns round there, rifles pegged to the walls or a shotgun, maybe, but he couldn't recall any. He hadn't been especially interested in guns right then.

But he had to make sure, little as he dared to waste further time.

First, however, he went over and tried the outside door. The latch worked freely. It wasn't locked.

He closed it and went back to the desk, feeling in the corners against the wall. No rifles. No sawed-off. He went round the room's corners and still didn't find any. He guessed there just weren't any spare weapons around there.

He put his belt back on and stood a moment considering. He wished he could know for sure what that Mexican and Brush were doing. Probably straining their eardrums trying to hear him again. They didn't think they had got him or they'd be making more noise.

He went back to the street door and lifted the latch. He stopped short in the act of swinging it open. Boots and spurs sounded on the walk. There was a grumble of voices. Curly Bill's voice said: "Wyatt Earp ain't tellin' *me* where t' head in at!"

Whit let go of the latch like he'd grabbed up a rattler.

There wasn't any doubt they were coming in. Somebody's boots were on the steps already.

Whit whirled like a cat and went back down the corridor.

He slipped into his cell, pulled the door shut after him, went across to the wall that had once held a window and stood there a bit with his head cocked, listening. He heard the street door open, heard Bill's voice again. He ducked through the hole and stepped into the alley.

He crouched, cocked and watchful, but could make out nothing that would do him any good. He moved forward a little, getting away from the wall, putting his feet down carefully, not settling his weight until sure of his footing. It would be fatal to make any sound out there now.

He threw a look toward the street but saw nothing against it. He looked back down the alley but saw nothing there save unrelieved blackness. It seemed utterly empty but he dared not believe that. Somewhere up there in the inky shadows Brush would be waiting with that kill-hungry Mexican.

He heard a grunt near the alley-mouth. "I'm gittin' plumb tired of this," somebody grumbled, and somebody else said,

"Shut up!" Then silence closed over the alley again.

But Whit knew by those words he would not get out that way.

Then he heard Curly Bill's voice come through the window hole. "Where the heck've they got to? What's become of that pilgrim? Git a lamp lit, Crowder."

The only chance he had left was to get past the star-packers. He could never hope to slip past them without noise to cover his passing. He couldn't stay where he was, because as soon as that lamp flared inside the jail, its light, pouring out through that broken wail, would disclose his whereabouts to all and sundry.

Brush's voice, very sure, reached dryly out of the blackness. "Throw down your gun an' come out, Slim."

Whit held his tongue.

"Last chance," Brush called. "I won't give you another."

Quite a joker, Ben Brush, but Whit didn't laugh. It was lucky for Brush Whit did *not* have a gun, for by the look in his eyes, he'd have used it. He sensed right away what the marshal was up to. Brush had geared that talk for the bystanders. He wanted to make sure they'd fire at Whit on sight.

"Crowder! Ain't you found thet lamp?"

That was Curly Bill's snarl coming out of the jailhouse.

Whit waited no longer. It was now or never.

He settled down on his bootheels, felt around in the trash till he got a tin can and the neck of a bottle. Swaying back from the waist, he flung them, one after the other, just as hard as he could into that black murk before him.

He heard them strike, saw a leaping flame cleave the yonder darkness as Corrado's gun blasted holes in the night. In the uproar Whit moved. He went fast and far, straight into that murk Corrado's gun was blasting. Twenty strides he went, then abruptly stopped, his outstretched hand recoiling from the cold and unexpected touch of metal, twin tubes that at once swayed away from him. In that moment, he heard a man's breath sharply pulled through his teeth.

Whit dived wickedly forward, crashing headlong into Brush who cursed and tried to bring up his shotgun. Whit rushed against him and kept desperately crowding him, slugging with every bit of strength he had.

With a clatter the shotgun fell out of

Brush's hands and Whit knew at once Brush had reached for his belt gun. He swung his fist at Brush's head and his chest struck Brush's shoulder, and he drove his left fist into Brush's wind.

But it wasn't enough. Brush was tough and tricky, long schooled in the art of roughhouse fighting. He fell away from Whit's blow and brought a knee up savagely, and Whit Brand yelled and dropped his hands in swift agony. But the rasp of Brush's gun coming out of leather sent him forward again, staggering into Brush, driving Brush back with his crippled weight, reaching for Brush's gun hand, striving to grip it before Brush could bring the gun into line.

Luck favored him for a moment, and he did catch hold of it and clung to it desperately, sick and dizzy though he was, while they swayed back and forth across the insecure footing.

But it was only a question of time and Whit knew it. Brush's other fist found his face and kept striking it and the rank taste of blood was in Whit's mouth. And over and above the stomp and thud of the struggle, through their grunts and their panting, he could hear Corrado coming through the trash.

Whit could not guard his face from punishment. Brush had the range and his blows kept landing. Whit knew if he ever let go of Brush's wrist he was done for.

Then a flare of light poured out of the jailhouse and, in its reflection, Whit saw Brush's face. He drove his free fist against Brush's jaw with all the strength of desperation and felt Brush lurch back in a weak-legged stagger. In that fragmentary quiet he heard the stomping of a horse and a part of his mind placed the sound to the left of him; and then Brush ripped free with a muttered curse.

Whit hurled himself aside as Brush's gun went off. A savage hand grabbed Whit's shoulder and Whit's spurred heel got hung up in the trash and he went down, Corrado with him, the Mexican clawing for Whit's throat. Whit ripped a spur across the Mexican's shins, and as the deputy's hands fell away, rolled clear over, knocking Brush down as the man fired again. But before Whit could whirl to his feet, Corrado had him.

Lightning fast, Corrado's elbow slid under Whit's back and Whit knew right then that he was finally done.

14

QUEER INTERLUDE

If her father was right and Kane had really been trying to oust Brush from office, Taisy could not see what this trip would avail them. But the colonel had made up his mind to go, and little as she cared for Kane's company, she had no intention of letting him go alone. In spite of her scoffing remarks to the contrary, Taisy was still much too scared he had been right about Brush.

She would have liked to believe he had been right about Brand. The man was attractive; she had at once felt drawn to him. They could hardly have found a man more likely to inspire trust. How well she could recall him, how clearly she remembered the clean curve of his cheek, the directness of his gaze, his amazed confusion when he'd found she did not believe him. A secret pleasure over the purposeful way he had knocked Brush down still warmed her. It was a pity she could not trust him — but she dared not. Too many queer things had been happening.

She thought of him, though, as they walked toward the house Kane had built at the faraway end of the mesa.

The vast loneliness of that harsh hill country was encouraging to thought and, in a girl, to dreaming. Taisy, motherless these many years, had done her share of such dreaming. It was not too surprising that she should find the young stranger remarkably like a certain figure her fancies had been much concerned with.

His eyes were the same — like smoky sage with the first flash of dawnlight breaking across it. And there was something else, too, that set him apart from other men she had known, though she could not quite decide what it was. Not his clothes, certainly. Not his dusty boots with their bright flashing spurs. Not the fierceness he'd displayed in his attack on Ben Brush — these things were common in Taisy's experience.

Perhaps, she thought, it was his quietness, a certain charm of manner with which his eyes had searched her. She liked his soft Texas drawl, the clean white flash of his teeth.

There'd been something naïve and engaging about him, something frank and boyish. But those, she reminded herself, suddenly frowning, must have been the very attributes that had earned him his part in Brush's little drama that evening. Curly Bill could never have expected to fool them with a man like Sandy King or John Ringo.

She quit thinking of Whit then and thought instead of this man her father set so much store by, this Comstock Kane who owned the camp's richest mine. And again she wondered why she couldn't quite like him. She had liked him well enough for a while; she had sat and talked with him many an evening when he had come, ostensibly to call on her father. She had been enthralled by the stories he'd told her of far-off places, of Chicago and Abilene, Fort Worth and Tascosa. She had marveled at the things he had told her — of water that ran from taps in the houses, water you didn't have to pump to get started, of great buildings where he'd watched folks play-act, where everyone dressed in fine clothes like himself and the women went clad in fine silks and laces, with furs at their throats and precious gems on their fingers.

She had liked him well enough until that

night. That night when he'd taken her in his arms — how vividly it all came back to her, each embarrassing facet of that hateful scene. It had been so unexpected, so unlooked for, so uncalled for. With his arms tightly round her, she had stood stiffly still, held rigid by the look in his glowing eyes. The same suffocation again came over her now. "What did you say?" she had whispered.

"I'm asking you to marry me. It doesn't have to be at once, if you're not willing — I could wait a little while. A couple of weeks, perhaps a month, till you get used to the idea."

"But, Comstock —" she'd said. And all the words had fled out of her. She'd tried pretending he was joking but he wouldn't have it that way. "I didn't know —"

"You must have guessed. I've been coming to see you pretty frequently, haven't I?"

"Yes, I know. But —"

"Well, you understand now. I want to marry you, Taisy. I want to make you my wife. You'll have furs and fine dresses — you'll be a somebody round here, the most important woman in this part of the country. You can —"

"But, Mister Kane. . . . Really —"

"Mr. Kane? Ah, Taisy!" He'd held her

off and smiled at her in that easy, amused way of his. "Really, my dear, your modesty is a little out of place at the moment. Stop acting like a child and set the day — See! I'm panting for you. I'm beside myself. Be a good girl now and set the day."

Taisy drew a long breath. "You must believe me, Comstock. I never dreamed —"

"Then I'll show you," he had said, and released her hands. He'd taken her suddenly, forcefully into his arms and kissed her full and hard on the lips. . . .

Resentment poured through her again, just as the memory. She had pulled away from him. She remembered how his face had darkened, how his mouth had gone tight and quivered a little as it always did when he became really angry. But it was only for an instant; then the old look was back and his eyes were teasing her.

"I guess that should show you I mean it." He was watching her closely behind his smiling regard. She could feel his green eyes digging into her, but his voice, when he spoke, held the same suave sureness it always had.

"This will tickle your Dad. I know he's always been hoping we might travel double, Taisy. Perhaps I'll think of some way to make that mine of his pay — pay enough, anyway, to justify his faith in it. It's a pitiable sight to see a man chase a rainbow all his life the way he has."

She'd stood silent, confused, unable to find the right words, vaguely frightened. She didn't know why she should feel frightened of Comstock. He had come to her then and once more, circumspectly, had taken her into his arms, briefly squeezed her. She hadn't offered any resistance. "Think it over," he'd said, and patted her shoulder. "We'll consider it settled. You can give me the date when you've made up your mind."

She had managed to avoid him pretty well ever since then — had managed, at least, not to be with him alone. Something had warned her not to let him guess this was intentional; she had concealed her real feelings behind a show of light banter. It made her feel like a hypocrite and the need for such dissembling made her furious. Other men had paid court to her, a lot of others had tried to, but with all the other men she'd been able to be herself. None had instilled in her the feeling Com Kane did.

They found Kane at home. His housekeeper, an angular woman in her forties, with a sniff in her voice and a pair of hawk eyes, told them Kane was in conference with his mine superintendent and, ushering them into the parlor, went off to apprise the great man of their presence. It was the first time Taisy had been in Kane's house and she spent the time looking around her with interest.

He didn't keep them long. Almost at once he appeared in the doorway. His eyes lighted up as they rested on Taisy, and he came straight to her, taking her hands warmly into his own. "Well," he said, "this *is* a treat! Sit down — sit down. No apologies necessary. I'm delighted to see you, Colonel."

He spoke to the colonel but his eyes stayed on Taisy.

He was dressed much as usual, like a dude straight out of the catalogue, with a stock to his shirt and fine lace at the sleeves which, taken in conjunction with his bottle-green coat and sleek trousers, gave him quite a dashing appearance.

"No, no," he said, "don't trouble yourself," as the colonel would have offered further apologies. "Always glad to be of use to my friends — delighted," he said, his handsome face watching Taisy and smiling.

The colonel broke at once into an agitated discourse concerning the subject of their call, explaining to Kane the singular events which he believed had culminated in Brand being jailed. Taisy sat across from them on the elegant sofa. She didn't think Kane too interested in her father's account of recent events but perhaps her judgment was colored by the frequency of Kane's admiring glances in her direction.

When old Jim had finished Kane sat back in his chair with his fingertips thoughtfully pressed together. "There's a chance, of course, that this stranger, Brand, is standing in with Brush . . . that they're up to something. Let me think a moment."

Several times his glance shuttled over to Taisy; he did not seem to be too wrapped up in the colonel's problems. She knew a bitter impulse to spring up and stamp out of there, but something in his regard suddenly stopped her. She tried to get up and couldn't; his eyes wouldn't let her. She sank back on the sofa, inexplicably frightened.

"I'll go with you, of course," Kane said smoothly to the colonel, "though I hardly think it will prove of much use. I have no influence with the man, I'm afraid. He knows I've brought pressure to try and get rid of him — I have made no secret of it. The man's obviously a crook. Everyone knows he's in league with Curly Bill and the rest of these ruffians. But I'll go with you, Colonel. That's the least I can do."

Taisy gathered her skirts and got up off the sofa.

Kane stood up at once. "No — you mustn't go yet. If we're successful at all, a little longer won't matter; the young man is probably perfectly comfortable. I've — ah — ordered some refreshments. . . ."

"Really —" began Taisy; but he wouldn't hear of their leaving until they'd sampled his tea.

"A special blend," he smiled. "I have it shipped from New Orleans — a most piquant taste. Do sit back and be comfortable. We'll not lose much time. If you'll excuse me a moment I'll have the buckboard brought round. . . ."

In the end Taisy had to sit down again and control her impatience while the frozen-faced housekeeper served them cakes and the tea from New Orleans. But as soon as they were finished and the "special blend" had been suitably complimented, Taisy jumped to her feet. "I really must go," she said nervously. "It's nearly suppertime and nothing's ready — the crazy miners will wreck the place. Come, Dad!" she cried, hastily tying her bonnet strings.

Kane drew on his gloves and picked up his tall beaver.

His handsome buckboard, resplendent with varnish, stood waiting at the steps behind a showy pair of bays.

Kane helped Taisy in with another of his smiles and a deal more solicitude than Taisy found needful. Her father climbed in, and Kane walked around and got in on the other side; after first unsnapping the weights from the horses. He picked up the lines and cracked his whip with a flourish.

"I've a little errand to do before we go over there, if you can indulge me," he told the colonel as the team set off at a spanking canter.

Taisy listened to her father's agreement, and as soon as he finished speaking, she said, "I've got to get back to the restaurant. You've no idea what a task it is playing cook to a campful of —"

"That's all right," Kane said without turning. "I'll drive you straight there."

And he let the bays go. They arrived in good season, and after he had helped her down and enigmatically watched her go up

165

the steps, he put on his hat and climbed back with the colonel. He turned the team with a practiced hand and pulled them up before McConaghey's bar.

"Now," he said, "I shan't be inside but a minute. I'm meeting a — Say!" he exclaimed, eyeing the colonel in surprise. "Maybe you ought to meet this fellow — engineer with a real nose for ore. Wouldn't hurt to have him look at your mine. He works at Tyrone; he's with the Burro Mountain outfit. . . ."

He broke off, frowning. His glance swept the loafers on the porch of McConaghey's, among them Ira McLown, who had been Wainright's partner.

"Trouble is," he said, lowering his voice and speaking guardedly, "this fellow isn't supposed to be over here right now. He only came down here to do me a favor. It would never do for him to be seen in public with a couple of mine owners. Might cost him his job. Someone might recognize him and pass the word back."

He sat thoughtful a moment and then pulled up his chin as though he'd come to a decision. "Tell you what you do, Colonel. You wait here a few minutes, then put on a show of being disgusted, and get down and walk off. Go over and wait out back of Jack

Dall's. I'll try to get him to come over and talk with you. Won't do any harm — he might locate that vein for you. Then we'll go over and get to work on Brush. What do you say?"

"Well —" Wainright said.

"Sure, it's too good a chance to pass up." Kane nodded. "You go ahead then. We'll meet you over in back of Jack's place. Give me a couple of minutes before you start off now."

With a reassuring smile in the gathering dusk, Kane slapped the colonel's shoulder and went on up the steps, nodding briefly to McLown as he stepped through the door.

Ten minutes later he came out again, got into his buckboard and drove off toward home.

15

VALLEY OF THE SHADOW

Locked in Corrado's strangling grip, with the deputy's knee in the small of his back, Whit saw Ben Brush fling round and come at him. Starlight danced off the barrel of Brush's pistol, off his gleaming teeth and out of his gloating eyes. He came without sound, like a springing panther. Whit tried to twist clear but Corrado held him. Corrado's breath was hot on his neck as the man bunched his muscles to exert more pressure.

The man had the strength of a rock crusher. A red fog whirled before Whit's eyes and he heard one yell of pain go up. The will that had braced his body snapped and his shape went slack and that was when the marshal struck.

Thrust off balance by Whit's sudden crumpling, Corrado lurched forward full into Brush's blow. Pulled forward by Whit's weight, Corrado took Brush's gun barrel between the shoulders. All the breath belched out of him and he dropped over Whit's body like a falling tent.

Pain clawed at Whit's chest like a twisting knife. "You fool! Kill that lamp!" Curly Bill's voice roared, and darkness rushed over the alley again, but not before Whit had seen a horse's tied shape, the horse he'd heard restively stamping. It was beyond the wire fence stretched across the alley ten feet away.

Whit didn't think Brush would fire with Corrado on top of him, but there was nothing to stop Brush from hammering his brains out with the barrel of that pistol. He tried to listen for Brush, tried to guess the man's location, but the alley was filled with the mutterings and calls of the men pouring into its mouth off the street.

He tried to squirm clear of the unconscious deputy. If he could reach that horse —

But Brush must have heard him. Just as he flung Corrado off himself, a tongue of light leaped out of the blackness. Another and yet one more vivid flash flung gangrenous light across the torn shadows. Something clouted Whit's hand — his good right one — and one of Brush's slugs slammed into a can not a foot from Whit's head and sent it clattering.

Dust and death made a smell in that gun stench, and the grating ends of a broken rib made it hard for Whit to keep from groaning and giving his position away again. He could hear Ben Brush shoving loads in his pistol and the men from the street kept yelling questions.

He gritted his teeth and came up on an elbow and, half sick with pain, thrust down his left hand and levered his chest up out of the trash. That gave off some noise and, six feet away, Ben Brush fired again. The slug ricocheted off a rock behind him and went screeching off through the darkness.

Those men crowding in off the street through the trash were making more noise than a trainload of elephants. Brush yelled at them viciously. But Whit had a knee propped under himself now. He was drawing his other foot up to rush Ben when he felt glass snap beneath the braced knee.

He couldn't choke back the groan. He knew Brush heard it. The last vestige of caution went out of Whit then. He lurched to his feet and Brush's gun roared at him. He flung himself back from the whine of the bullet. He went staggering toward the fence at a drunken run, forgetful of the fence, his mind on the horse that was tied beyond it.

He went into it headlong, the bite of the barbed wires hurling him back full into Ben Brush who was plunging after him.

Both men went down in a thrashing tangle. Whit struck Brush across the face with his elbow. Brush drove a fist through Whit's broken rib; the pain of that blow was purest agony. But Whit slammed Brush backward and tore himself free. Again he tried for the fence but the marshal tripped him.

He fell heavily, gasped, tried to get up and crawl, but Brush was on him with the lunge of a tiger. The breath was half knocked out of Whit and the pain of that grating rib made him retch. Again Brush slammed into him. He hit Whit's head with his fists like a hammer. Whit drove a knee in the marshal's belly and Brush rolled off him with a strangled whimper.

Half dazed, sick and gagging, Whit dragged himself to his feet and heard Brush come off the ground close by. He tried to turn and was that way, half turned, when Brush's fist hit him again.

Even as he fell Whit thought about the blow with a blurred kind of wonder. It took a pretty fierce blow to knock a man

171

sprawling that way, but Whit didn't feel it. He didn't feel the ground either when it came up and slapped him. He guessed he was beyond feeling anything till some crazy fool started screeching his head off and it came to him suddenly that it was himself doing the screaming and that Brush was beside him trying to kick all his ribs out.

He tried to roll over, he tried to drag himself clear of those striking boots, and his left hand gratefully closed on something that cleared his head like a dash of cold water. He knew then why Brush was kicking him. He knew then why, before, Brush had used his fists. When that fence had flung Whit back into the marshal, Brush had let his gun get away from him. It was Brush's gun now that was in Whit's hand.

With that gun in his fist, it took all Whit's will to fight down the terrible urge that came over him, the wicked desire to kill this man as he would a snake. Brush deserved no better, and Whit's fevered blood, all the black rage that was bottled inside him, cried out for him to do it, at once, to shoot Brush down as he would a wolf.

But he mastered the impulse. He wasn't built that way. Twice he half raised the gun

172

as the man's black shape hulked over him, but each time the inherent goodness in Whit stopped him. He shook like a leaf. The butt of the gun in his bullet-torn hand was sticky with blood, his thoughts incoherent because of the burning agony that tore through his chest. But, crook or not, Ben Brush was still marshal. He still wore the law's tin pinned to his shirtfront, and Whit called painfully: "I've got a gun in my hand, Brush. You better get out of here."

But Brush, if he heard him, plainly didn't believe it. Whit felt him glare through the darkness, saw the roll of his shoulders, heard his boots start forward. "When I leave this place I'll be draggin' you with me — dead," Brush said, and swung his boot back.

Hardly knowing what he did, Whit slammed out with the pistol. The barrel struck Brush's shin with a meaty impact. The marshal reeled away cursing, went single-footing round in an off-balance circle as Whit rolled over and came up on his knees. "Git, damn you — *git!*" he cried. And, half wild with pain, he squeezed the trigger.

Nothing happened at all. In the blackest despair Whit hopelessly realized the gun was empty or clogged with dirt. Brush had heard that click — his shape had rooted. One short laugh fell out of him. He was coming now. Whit understood that, and shuddered.

Only exhaustion kept Whit at it; he was too licked to run, too beat to try. He had never got hold of a gun so heavy. He wondered what fool had put glue on its handle. It was a slippery stickiness between his numb fingers. With a kind of wild anger he kept squeezing the trigger; and the gun went off.

That report almost tore the gun from Whit's hand. The marshal cursed, Whit saw his shape whirl through the powder-streaked shadows, heard his boots racketing as he plunged through the trash.

Whit clawed to his feet and stumbled toward the fence, groping for it with his good left hand while the alleyway rang with Brush's noise and men's shouting. The sharp barbs ripped his clothes as Whit floundered through and a wire-snagged spur threw him flat on his face. He hadn't the strength to get up again, and so he crawled, like a crab, toward the sound of the pony.

The sight of him alarmed it.

The horse blew through his nostrils and reared back, frightened, scared of the blood smell and the strangeness of the thing that moved like a snail, toward it. And it came over Brand with a forlorn kind of wonder that this was the end, that he was done now and finished. Not in this world would he ever be able to get his spent self up into that saddle, not even if the horse would stand there and let him.

He opened his eyes and saw flame before them. Beautiful it was, with brilliant blues and blended scarlets rimming a center of rich yellow pollen. It took him some time to discover this miracle was only a match held in cupped hands before him. He heard a man's hoarse oath and a smothered cry that could only have come from the throat of a woman. Then the man's voice said, "This has got me beat. Take a look at him, Taisy — ever see him before?"

There was a long-drawn-out gasp, and then the girl's voice said: "It's that gun fighter Dad was — But I knew they . . . Ira, *look!* Is that blood —"

"He's comin' out of it," the man said. He dropped his match. Strong hands helped Whit to his feet a little roughly, one hand keeping hold of him as though he might bolt. "Keep yore eye on him," the man said. "I'm goin' to fetch Brush."

"Brush!" cried the girl; and that name roused Whit as nothing else could have.

"My God," he breathed. "Mister —"

But the girl said quickly, "You can't do that, Ira! This is one of Brush's men! He's apt to —"

"Brush's?" the man said. "He must of been in that gun fight — you reckon Jim shot him?"

Whit could hear the dim sound of yelling voices. The girl must have heard them too, for she said with a note of urgency: "You've got to get him out of here! Quick, Ira — *hurry!*"

The man stroked his jaw with his free hand, and pondered. "You say this feller is one of Brush's men? I don't call him to mind."

"He's the man that made out to be saving my father — the fellow Dad thought they took off to jail. Don't you know? I told you. That's why we —"

"You ain't thinkin' straight, girl; you've got to calm yourself down. Jim couldn't of been mixed in this — it's like I told you. Jim never went near that jail at all. He —"

"You don't understand!" the girl cried. She sounded desperate, frightened. "It's a part of the trap — oh, I know it is! How right Dad was! He said Brush meant to kill him and I didn't believe it — I didn't think Brush would go for Dad so open — I couldn't see the sense in it —"

"There ain't none," the man said, but he didn't sound too sure of it. "Anyway, if Brush wanted to git rid of Jim for some reason, he sure wouldn't of tried nothin' that brash an' open. It ain't Brush's way. Ben plays the cards a heap closer to his chest."

"But he *is!*" Taisy said. "And I know what they're after — you know yourself! Or you ought to! You were part of it."

"Me! You're crazy, girl!"

"It all started," Taisy said, "when Kane bought your interest in the Luckybug Lode. Why would a man like Kane buy into a mine that he knew to be worthless? Don't you see it?"

The man shook his head. "I don't guess I do. It sounds —"

But the girl didn't let him finish. "Oh, we've all been so blind! Because Dad never found anything worth while, we all sort of took it for granted that he never would find anything — but he did!" she cried. "And Comstock Kane knows it! That's why he bought you out. That's why he's been wanting to marry me! When he saw I wouldn't have him he hit on this plan. He bought you out — that gave him a half-interest. Now he's done something to Dad."

"You don't know that. It's plumb foolish. I was there. I was right there settin' on McConaghey's porch an' Comstock Kane had nothin' to do with it. Kane was inside when yore dad got outen that buckboard an' went stalkin' off toward Jack Dall's place."

"And isn't that where we heard all that shooting?"

"Mebbe so. Hard to tell. But this feller come out of that alley —"

"It was a running fight. Or meant to be thought one. You know yourself how —" She quit and whirled on Whit fiercely. "Where is my father? What have you done with him?"

Whit didn't know what she was talking about. He hadn't been trying to keep up with their jawing. "How could I be knowin' about your father, ma'am, when I only just now got away from that jail?"

"Don't lie!" Taisy flared. "You've never been in that jail!"

Whit looked at her wonderingly. He said dryly, "I wisht I was right, ma'am."

He staggered back with a burst of lights in his eyes. He put out a hand but he knew he was falling. It was the last thing he knew for a considerable interval.

Ira said, shocked: "You're damn rough with a man. You shouldn't ort to of struck —"

"It's all they know." Taisy forced all feeling out of her voice. "You've got to be tough with that kind of man, Ira."

She was sick, though, inside.

Why couldn't this man have been different? Why couldn't he have been the kind of man he had appeared to be, young and generous and wholesome? — not a gun-slinging bravo whose soul could be hired for a handful of silver. Why was the world such a hard place to live in?

Taisy choked back a sob and said, "Get him out of here. If you can't see through this yourself, trust my judgment."

She didn't realize what emotion had done to her voice, how sharply the pitch of it had brought Ira's head up. She didn't notice how queerly he stood there eyeing her, or the way he looked down at the man on the floor. She was fighting for calmness, to preserve her values, for the will to do what her mind thought she ought to. And her mind didn't think she ought to fiddle with Brand at the possible expense of her father's safety.

She mustn't let this sneaking liking for an unknown drifter jeopardize all her father had worked for. Even admitting his attraction — and she didn't intend to — Brand was just one other tough gun-hung saddle tramp Brush had employed to further Kane's purpose: the acquirement or control of the Luckybug Lode!

For that was the answer to all this violence. It was the reason Kane had bid for her hand in marriage — you couldn't tell Taisy differently. It had prompted his purchase of Ira's half-interest in the Wainright mine. Kane wasn't fooling her any more than this Brand was. She had her eyes open. She had even considered McLown for a moment with an edge of this new-found awareness; Ira had, after all, supplied Kane's first chance. He had given the Planchas boss a half-owner's voice in the private affairs of the colonel's mine.

But she dismissed this suspicion of Ira impatiently. She had known old Ira McLown for years. His career and her father's had been in many ways parallel, their meanderings had taken them over much the same ground; and she remembered how he used to sit and, with many fierce faces and appropriate gestures, tell terrible tales of his early adventures. It was hard to suspect such a man of trickery. For Taisy, it was well nigh impossible.

But this tolerance did not extend to new faces. She was ready to believe any evil of Brush; he was a soft-footed man with sly eyes and no laughter. It had long been common talk in that camp that Brush owed his job to Curly Bill's influence, and any man who'd lap crumbs from an outlaw's table would be quite capable of biting that hand if a shift in conditions made ingratitude profitable. She had no illusions about Brush, that was certain.

It was just unfortunate, she thought, that a prank of fate should have led McLown to fetch Whit there, thinking he was her father. Though how Ira, even in the dark and under the stress of excitement, could have been so mistaken she could not fathom. It was one of those things, and she let it go at that. But they must get him away before Brush found him there. Brush had probably connived to fool Ira that way. He could make out a good case against them, or at least throw discredit on Taisy's judgment, if he could show she was sheltering a man whom this evening he had publicly arrested. Taisy wasn't too sure of the motives behind this but she needed no crystal to know they were bad ones.

McLown straightened up and gave a tug at his hat brim. "What do you want I should do with him?"

"You'd better take him back and leave him there where you found him."

"They'll hev missed thet horse before this," Ira protested. "They had him tied out back of thet jailyard fence."

"They put it there for him to get away on," Taisy said inconsistently.

"They might of figured he would take it," Ira said with a sniff, "but he sure wouldn't of got mighty far on thet critter. It's thet cart horse of O'Dade's what he's been workin' on his scraper."

"And O'Dade is one of Comstock Kane's drivers!" Taisy cried. "What did you do with it?"

"Put him out back in thet patch of syca-mores. He won't go far — I tied him."

Taisy glanced through the gloom at the man on the floor. She chewed her lip ner-vously. If the man was hurt — but she mustn't think of that; no telling what those wretches had done to her father! They must get Whit Brand out of there. At any moment Ben Brush might come storming. . . . "Fetch the horse to the door and we'll load him onto it. You can lead it off into the brush some place and then, if he's found, it won't involve us."

"We ort to take another look. He seemed —"

"Let me do the thinking. You go fetch the horse," Taisy said, and he took a long look at her, shrugged, and went out.

16

THE BRAND OF CAIN

Taisy stood with the door held ajar and listened to the things which the night had to tell her, to the far remote calling of men's lifted voices, to the racket of a horse in the canyon. A faint wind came up with that sound off the water and the stamp mill's thunder was blessedly silent, and a man on the street called, "All right," to someone. Taisy closed the door and looked down at the drifter.

She wished again, with all her heart, this man had been different — had at least, in some part, justified her Dad's faith in him. If the colonel hadn't been so determined to help him. . . . She pulled up her chin and swung away from Brand blindly. She must scour from her mind this saddle bow slim with his gay kindly eyes and his black-hearted treachery. There was no good in him. He was a gun-handy drifter admirably shaped to Brush's needs! Was she a child to be taken in by such shifts, by such puerile deceptions as torn clothes and a pounded face? No doubt he had been well paid for it, and would have been better paid if he had managed to fool them. Let him stew in his own duplicity! He would find she wasn't that simple.

Every aspect of the plot was very clear to her now. Her father *had* struck it rich. Their mine *was* a bonanza, and somehow Comstock Kane had unearthed the truth — had even managed to discover it ahead of her father. Here was plainly what had inspired the man's hateful ardor — Yes! and Curly Bill too! Bill must also have learned. She should not have been surprised to find them working together; it would not be the first time avowed enemies had quit squabbling and pooled their energies in the hope of quick profit!

Bronc sound roused her from her thoughts and she stiffened. Alarm rushed through her. She had a sinking feeling it was Ben Brush coming. She gave a small, quick sigh of anxiety and ran to snatch down her father's rifle. Then Ira came in and closed the door.

"By grab," he panted, "they're after him, all right! Half the men in this camp is out beatin' the bushes an' Brush an'

Corrado is workin' with lanterns tryin' t' pick up his sign."

They both whirled as Brand groaned and tried to get himself upright. Ira reached down and helped him, held a steadying hand underneath Whit's elbow. "You'll have to get me out of here," Whit mumbled in a voice that seemed to come out of his boots. "I guess I heard most of what you told her. I wouldn't want to get you folks in no trouble. . . ."

Taisy glared, trying to bite back the words that threatened to leap out and blast him. Trouble, indeed!

McLown said, "You hurt much?"

"I'll make it," Whit grunted, but his voice didn't encourage any belief in his statement. He put up a good act. Taisy gave him credit.

She thought bitterly of her father, vanished without a trace, whose plight was directly traceable to this man; and decided nothing she could wish would be bad enough for him. She did not for a minute think her slap had really dropped him — he'd fallen in the hope it would be to his advantage to do so. She could imagine the hateful grin on his face now.

She wished she were a man. A man would know how to handle him.

"I'll be all right," he said. "I got creased a couple times gettin' out of that alley. . . ." His voice went thin and faded.

It was insult to injury that he could act such a lie. Taisy cried: "How can you stand there and say those things?" Her cheeks burned with anger, her hands itched to strike him. "What have you done with my father? What *have* you?" She knew an increasingly tight and desperate feeling. "If I were only a man!"

"Miz' Taisy, ma'am," Whit said hoarsely, "believe me! I swear I don't know what's happened to your Dad! I been in that jail —"

"If you had been in that jail you would still be in there! I'm not a child — I know what you're up to! If you had been in that jail you couldn't have got out unless Brush let you."

"You're right, ma'am. That's right. That's exactly what happened. Brush an' that Mexican of his rigged up a jail break so they could have me outside where killin' me later wouldn't make them no trouble."

"A very likely story!"

Whit said, "If you would look at me, ma'am —"

"To see the marks of your conflict? Ben Brush is no fool! If that story were true you wouldn't be standing here. You'd be gone from this camp. Or dead in that alley."

"I come mighty near bein' jest that," Whit mumbled, and his breathing grew suddenly quick and shallow like he was about to pretend to go off in a faint again.

Taisy's lips wouldn't curl. She was too angry for that, too worried with fear for her father to waste more time bandying words with the fellow.

She whirled away, swung toward Ira. "Get him out of here — hurry!" Her voice cracked and broke on a note of near panic. "We've got to find Dad! Oh, hurry, Ira — hurry!"

"I'll take a look at him first."

There came the rasp of a match. The flare of it traveled across their faces. "My Gawd!" McLown said. "He do look beat up."

"Of course he looks beat up! Those men are not fools; they don't think we are — quite. We're beholden to this fellow — they want our hearts to go out to him. That first play didn't work so now Brush tries out a new stunt — can't you see it, Ira?" She cried out impatiently: "It's all of a piece with Kane buying you out. Dad's in bonanza. Kane found it out. He'll do what he has to — he wants —"

"You say Jim's in bonanza!"

McLown couldn't believe it. He stared at her stupidly, dropping his hand from the drifter. "Oh, damn!" he growled suddenly as Brand's sagging shape started floorward again. "Here — help me, Taisy — the durn fool's gone agin. Git a light. Cover —"

"It's a trick," Taisy cried. "Watch out."

"Hell, it ain't no trick. The guy's been shot — I got blood all over me. Cover thet window an' git a light lit so's I kin see what I'm doin'."

She could hear Ira easing Whit onto the floor. She felt sure Whit was stalling, giving Brush time to get there and discover them hiding him in the Lone Star's back room with no light on.

Distracted, bewildered, sick with dread for her father, Taisy snatched a blanket from the bed and threw it over the window. The window faced nothing but the chaparral-dotted mesa now hidden in darkness, but half the town could be crouched out there waiting. Brand had not been there long — not over twenty minutes, perhaps not more than half that, but that might be time and to spare for whatever new deviltry Brush had cooked up. Each tick of the clock, each fluttering heartbeat might herald his coming, might announce his arrival. Each new moment might bring him to the door with his face stretched wide in a leering grin.

Taisy found a match, hardly knowing what she did. She crossed the bare floor, hurrying over to the wall, and reached up to the lamp bracketed there. Lifting the chimney, she thrust her match at the wick and a warm yellow glow brought the room into focus. She flew to the outside door and barred it. She flung back to where Ira bent over the stranger.

She started back, sickened, horrified at the sight of him. She threw a shaking hand up before her eyes, but she had to look. She could not quite stop the cry that came out of her. Looking down at the wreck of what this man had been, she remembered her doubt with startled anger. No man would take what this man had to hang onto a job, to keep up a deception — she had to believe that. And when belief came it shamed her. The man was hurt.

Anger suddenly gave her strength.

"Oh, Ira!" she cried in a strangled voice, and her hands clutched his shoulders convulsively. "Ira," she whispered, "is he going to die?"

17

TIME FOR WONDER

Having seen how wrong she had been in her judgment, how far from the truth had been her suspicions of this man she had instinctively liked from the start, Taisy was quick to accept the obligations Whit's plight and presence now laid upon them. The thought of postponing their search for her father was no easy thing for her to consider, but if her choice was hard it was also swift, for this stranger's need was urgent. While Ira was getting Whit onto the bed and examining him, she built up the fire and put water to boil, made coffee, slashed open the mattress and dug out some batting and ripped a clean sheet into strips for bandages.

This display of efficiency, her instant acceptance of the situation with all of its grave and possible consequences, would have amazed Whit. She showed now a depth and fortitude, and understanding and capability, he would have found astounding in one of her years and erstwhile conduct.

She pawed round until she found a handful of cartridges of a caliber that would fit her father's rifle. She got out the belt gun he never wore and loaded it from the loops at Whit's waist. She went to the window, making sure the blanket completely covered it, for how could they know there was no one watching? And all the time she kept listening for Brush.

This was no reflection of her former suspicions. It was a foreboding strongly backed by logic. Sooner or later Brush would come there. He would remember the sequence Whit's advent had broken. He would guess right away Whit was holed up there. It became imperative they get him away. The old reasons still stood, they were strengthened. It would suit Brush well to catch Whit there.

What could she say? What could she do if Brush did come?

"Will he live?" she whispered to Ira again.

"I dunno — hold that pan closer, can't you? . . . He don't look none too good and that's a fact, by Gawd. He's lost plenty blood. Got a busted rib. Thet gash in the knee ain't so bad as she looks. Be all right ef we kin keep down infection. Thet hand's the worst; it ain't never goin' to be much good to him. Lucky ef he don't lose it, I reckon. Gimme some o' thet battin'."

When they had Whit's knee and hand wrapped up and had done all they could for the moment, Ira said, "There ain't nothin' we kin do about thet busted rib — we wouldn't dast call none o' them docs in here. We can't keep him here neither, an' it ain't goin' to do him no good to be moved."

"I really don't see how we can move him, Ira. . . ."

"We got to," McLown said. "They'll come here sure when they don't find his sign on none of them trails."

"But where can we take him — and *how?*"

"There's that — well, I got a idear where I kin take him. Be jest as well ef you don't know. I'll pack him up there soon as you shake together some grub. I shore hate to put him on a horse in his shape, but I reckon a wagon would be plumb easy to foller."

"But, Ira! That horse!" Taisy cried excitedly.

"Huh? Horse?" Ira blinked. "Y' mean that horse of O'Dade's? What about it?"

"Didn't you say it was hitched behind the jail yard fence?"

McLown nodded. "Looked to me like the critter had been put there deliberate."

"Then wouldn't they follow the tracks if you rode it off?"

"They may be follerin' 'em now," Ira said, looking rather apprehensively toward the door.

"Did you come straight here?"

"From thet alley? Yeah — well, I antigodled around some, kind of hopin' not to meet —"

Taisy said with conviction, "If you were to take that horse and ride it back across your tracks, and then keep right on going like you were Brand, clearing out, I bet they'd follow —"

"Do I look like a fool?" Ira growled at her irritably.

"But, Ira! You've got to — you've got to lead them off so I can get Brand out of here. . . ."

Ira gave it some study. He didn't appear enthusiastic. Eyeing her slanchways, he said, "You couldn't never cut it. He's too heavy fer a girl. S'pose he fell off — you wouldn't never git him on again. What ef he died on you? Nope, I'll hev to do it."

"But if you led them off I could take him in a wagon — Look! His eyes are open!"

Ira crossed to the bed.

Taisy moved to the stove, at once busying herself. She went over to the bed with a mug that was filled with steaming coffee, black and pungently laced with whisky.

She slipped a hand underneath Whit's shoulders, raising him up a little so he could drink. He tried to hitch himself up to help her, but his weakness, the slow response of his muscles, was like a knife in her, twisting, and she looked away to keep him from seeing the fear in her eyes. Her heart cried out, wanting to say something to him, but what were words? Would words heal his wounds? Would they banish the memory of the way she had acted — the things she had said?

He seemed to sense her thoughts; she could feel him watching her with his coal-black eyes in that battered face, but she could not meet them, and when she finally looked his mouth was tight, the lines of his lips grimly harsh, as his glance swept over his bandaged hand. He put nothing in words but that glance told the story. She could see that he knew and that the thought of it scared him.

She bent over him, bracing him, supporting him while he drank.

"Does it hurt bad, Whit?"

"I was thinkin'," he said, "about you, ma'am. You shouldn't ought to be mixin' into this thing. It's between me an' Brush. I think you better get out of here."

"You're in no shape to travel."

"Don't you fret about that. Just set that gun over here where it's handy. . . ."

She got up off the bed, making of his empty cup an excuse to go over to the stove where her too bright eyes wouldn't give her away. And yet all the while, even through the poignant terror of her thoughts, she kept listening for Brush, for the sound of his footfall, for the creak of the doorstep.

She looked desperately at Ira where he stood frowning moodily just beyond the stove.

Ira meant all right, he had a heart of gold. It wasn't his fault he had a jumpy mind that usually worked from a hung-up trigger. When his thoughts got around to it he would fully grasp some perfectly obvious facet of this business and go exploding into action like a ton of thawed dynamite. His mind was loping after something now.

Ordinarily Taisy would have tried to head it off, but now she was too harassed herself to question what was eating him. His mind, she saw, was miles away; her own mind wasn't too quick right then with so many things besetting it. She wasn't fooled by Whit's hardy words. With his gun hand mangled and swathed in those wrappings, he would not, by himself, have any part of a chance; he couldn't even run, not with that broken rib and bad knee. His words were a bluff designed to protect her. It humbled Taisy. It made it hard for her to hold back the tears.

"Great guns, Taisy!" Ira cried suddenly. "You was mentionin' Kane — you wasn't thinkin' *he* had any part in me losin' thet money, was you?"

Taisy sighed. "Why not? Who else knew you had it? If you didn't tell anybody Kane *must* have. What's happened to that free-drink hunter, Smith, that was always so friendly with Curly Bill's marshal? No one's seen him around since that night you were robbed."

"Well . . . but Smith wa'n't no friend of Comstock Kane's. Kane never knowed him."

"Brush did!"

Ira looked at her, startled. "Are you

sayin' Brush an' Kane worked thet deal to-gether?"

Taisy shrugged, turned away. She turned back to Whit Brand again and saw how the coffee had thawed out his nerve ends, increasing his awareness, brightening his eyes with the pain thus unloosed in him. She wished she could take that pain away from him.

She went toward him. "If you could think of anything more I could do —"

"That horse," he said. "Where's that horse I was tryin' for?"

Taisy, with sharply increased alarm, remembered. Ira had fetched him, left him outside the door. Brush would know at once if he saw that horse.

Whit said, "If you would get me up on him I could —"

"That's a damfool remark," Ira said with a snort. "Thet broke-down cart horse would git you caught afore you ever got clear o' this camp! Brush would —"

"Not Brush." Whit's smile was a grimace. "I put a slug into —"

"Then thet Corrado an' the rest of Bill's crowd'll be huntin' you clean from hell t' breakfast! You got t' hev help, boy."

Whit looked set to argue. He tried to get off the bed. Taisy went to him quickly.

"You've got to help *us*," she said. "We need you. We're depending on you to help us find Dad." She told him how she and her father had gone after Kane in an effort to get him released from the marshal, and how her father had vanished.

McLown broke in, taking up where she left off. "Then Kane came out. He wanted t' know where Jim was. I told him Jim had got tired of waitin', it seemed like, an' had gone traipsin' off toward the back of Jack Dall's. Kane looked surprised. He looked kind of put out. He didn't say nothin' though. He got into his rig an' drove off toward home."

Whit lay hunched on an elbow, watching her brightly. He wasn't going to die; he was going to get better. She wasn't sure of that thought but she hung onto it fiercely. "And then," she went on, "when Dad didn't come home and it began to get late I got pretty worried. Ira came by — this is Ira you're talking to — Ira McLown, he used to be Dad's partner till he sold out to Kane — and he told me what had happened. It wasn't like Dad. We'd gone up there to fetch Kane — why would he leave that way? We tried to find him. No one had seen him. He hadn't gone to Dall's — no one recalled seeing him after he got out of

Kane's buckboard. We went back out to Kane's but Kane wasn't there; he'd gone up to the mine, his housekeeper said. We came back to town. There was a lot of shouting and shooting somewhere over near the jail. Ira went off to see what was happening. I came home and then — Oh!" Taisy cried, "he's passed out again, Ira!"

"We better git busy. I'll go hunt up a wagon — pack some grub," Ira muttered, and left her.

While he was gone Taisy put on a man's flannel shirt and blue jeans. She put on a pair of boots and was tucking her hair up under a Stetson when Ira came back.

Ira said, "I been thinkin'. Thet horse of O'Dade's didn't tie himself out there in back o' thet jail — not a chance. Thet horse was put there. Ef Brand got out of thet jail the way he told us, Brush must've tied thet horse out there. Ef Brand got loose of 'em they figgered he would take it."

He scowled at Whit's battered face. "Mebbe they never even figgered t' stop him in thet alley. Mebbe they wanted him t' fork thet horse. Then, when they ketched him, there wouldn't be no doubt he was a pris'ner tryin' to give 'em the slip. . . . Tell you what you do. I'll put him in thet wagon an' you light out fer thet old line camp of Kralsey's. Ain't nobody usin' thet old shack now an' it ain't no place they'll be a heap apt t' think of. You take him out there. While you're a-doin' it I'll be ridin' O'Dade's nag hell west an' crooked. Ef they're figgerin' to git him by trailin' thet skate, I'll give 'em enough sign t' last 'em a lifetime!"

18

"GO AHEAD —
YELL YER HEAD OFF"

McLown fetched the buggy and carried
Whit out to it. Taisy made him as comfortable as she could and swathed him heavily
with blankets. They could still see lights
bobbing round in the chaparral. Ira said
they were beating his trail all right, that
he'd still plenty of time to head them away
from the Lone Star. "I'll git off in thet
brush an' make a hell of a racket an' thet
whole damn push'll go larrupin' after me.
When they do, you light out. It won't take
me long to lose 'em in this dark. I'll meet
you at thet cabin along about daybreak.
Watch yourself now," he said, and kneed
O'Dade's horse away.

Taisy fetched her sack of supplies from
the restaurant. She brought her father's
rifle and the six-shooter she had loaded
from Whit Brand's belt. She climbed in

beside Whit and worriedly waited till she heard Ira's promised commotion off yonder. There were yells, a rattle of gunshots. Taisy waited no longer. She caught up the reins, turned the horse in a roundabout way toward the one used road that led down off the mesa and up Turkey Creek toward the old Kralsey line camp.

Not until the camp's yellow lights were tiny gleams far behind was she able even to approximate comfort, and her mind was not easy then. There were too many unexplained things to be thought of. There was her father's disappearance, the uncertainty of Brand's condition. She was unsettled in her mind; she couldn't quite put her finger on anything, but the unease, the grim foreboding which so long had gripped her seemed suddenly to have doubled.

It was silly to fret, she told herself irritably. She was being a goose. Brush had not burst into — Was he dead, then? Had Whit killed him? She could not imagine Ben Brush being dead. She should be thankful Brush's men had not stopped her; they must all have torn off after Ira. What if they caught him? They'd be furiously mad at the way he had tricked them. In their wrath — but she would not think of that. Ira knew the risk, Ira'd not let them catch him. Few men knew these hills as Ira McLown did. It had been smart of him to pick a place like Kralsey's. The old line shack was in an isolated part of the Cherrycow range; they could hide Whit there until his wounds healed. No one ever went out there now.

She kept to the stage road till she came to the turn-off. It was little more than a couple of ruts through the brushes. She turned the horse into them, drove a few yards and stopped where the buggy was well concealed by oak brush. She got down then and did what she could in the darkness to obliterate the tracks where their wheels left the road. She took one of the blankets off Whit and tied it onto the rear of the buggy in the hope that it might help to hide their sign.

There wasn't any moon. It was a cold, still night and this was a trail long unused since the Kralseys had given up trying to raise cattle in a country so gophered with mine shafts. In the awful silence the rattle of the buggy seemed unconscionably loud. The steady grind and squeak of the grease-less axle was enough to set one's teeth on edge, and Taisy expected to be stopped at every twist of the trail.

The trail was hardly better than a cow

track. Trying to follow its gyrations by the dim winking light of the faraway stars was a task to try the stoutest courage. Much of the time the way was all but impassable. Weeds and brush overgrew it rankly and Taisy frequently wondered if she still were following it. In other places the trail was so eroded and gutted she sometimes despaired of ever getting through it and she could not help but notice the bad effect of this traveling on Whit's condition. Fever had laid hold of him; his hands and face were like fire. He was beginning to mutter and mumble and Taisy eyed him alarmedly.

There were snatches of his talk that seemed almost lucid, like when he spoke of the finding of Smith's dead body, of his discovery of the picture and of McLown's empty wallet. Thus she came to know what had brought Whit there, how the picture of a girl had fetched him from the town of Helvetia in the Santa Ritas. "Sweet — that's what she is," Whit said. "Prettiest filly I ever set eyes on — prettier'n a little red wagon."

Again, he seemed to be talking about a horse, an old horse someone was beating. "All he needs," Whit said, "is a little kindness. Usin' the butt of a whip won't improve him — how'd you like to have me use it on *you?* I've sure got a mind to — Oh, you won't eh?" he shouted. "By grab, you put a price on him quick or I'll show you what a whip-end feels like!"

There were other times when he was trapped in the alley, and that was the worst, Taisy thought. That was terrible.

Some time after four the eastern sky began to pale and it was then she discovered she didn't know where she was. She wasn't on any trail. All about them barren ridges rose and fell from gulch to gulch. There was nothing familiar. When daylight broke gray and cold about them they were deep in a canyon the eroded walls of which rose sheer above the wind-tossed tops of trees that grew along a shallow creek. There was no longer any question about it. They were lost.

Taisy drove the buggy along the creek till further progress was stopped by an immense fallen tree. There was no way of getting the buggy past it. Nor could she discover any place where she could hide it, either. With despair like a lead weight dragging her hopes down, she tried to find some shelter she could get Whit into, some cave or something where she could make a fire to keep Whit warm and dry; but there was no such place.

She said, "Whit!" and somehow got him out of the buggy. He didn't quite fall but his arms, as he clung to the side of it, shook. She tried to take his weight on her own frail shoulders, but at the first step he took all the strength fell out of him and he went to his knees dragging her heavily with him. "This here's awright," he muttered, and his hands slipped away and he fell forward on his face.

There was nothing more she could do for him then. She left him there, after turning him over. She covered him with blankets and worriedly felt his forehead. His sweat wet her hand. She didn't understand that, for it was cold in the canyon. It was terribly cold, she thought with chattering teeth. But hadn't she heard somewhere that when you sweat you couldn't have fever? Maybe his fever was broken. He'll be all right now, she thought; but she was afraid to believe it.

She unharnessed the horse, led him off a little way and tied him with the reins to a tree, leaving him to browse. The sound of the creek was a restless gurgle, and to keep from hearing it, dog tired though she was, she set about gathering dead branches and stuff from which she might fashion some kind of a shelter. She knew she had to get Whit in out of the weather and she stopped long enough to build up a fire. Seeing he was sweating so, she was afraid he might chill and contract pneumonia. She built the fire close to him, building stones up behind it to throw back the heat.

She wouldn't let her mind consider the end of her predicament. Ira would find them. Ira knew those hills like the palm of his hand. When she didn't show up at the line camp he'd hunt her. He'd find the tracks of the buggy and follow them. . . .

She went back to the work of gathering branches, stopping now and again to bend over Whit and feel his forehead, hoping each time to find his eyes open and his mind functioning normally; looking each time to see his cheerful grin. But she never did. He continued to drowse in a kind of half-stupor, groaning, sometimes mumbling incoherently.

Toward noon she got some of her supplies from the buggy and threw together a meager meal. But she didn't eat much; she couldn't eat for thinking. Several times in his delirium Whit cried out for water. The day dragged endlessly. It wasn't so cold after the sun got high enough to look over

the lofty rim of the canyon; in the afternoon its light grew so fierce she had to let
the fire die and take the blankets off Whit.
Time and again she felt of his face and discovered with alarm that the fever was
building. She applied wet cloths to his face
but the fever continued; there was pain in
his breathing.

The sun slid toward the western horizon.
When it dropped behind the rim great
blue-black shadows at once gathered in the
canyon and the air chilled again and she
built the fire up and covered Whit with the
discarded blankets. As the darkness gathered and the shadows grew blacker, she
began to wonder, after all, whether Ira
would find them. He should have found
them long since. Had the marshal's men
caught him?

"It could work both ways," she said
abruptly, startling herself with the sound of
her voice. If Ira couldn't find her, surely
Brush and his ruffians, who'd no reason
even to look in that direction, would hardly
be apt to come across them there. Besides,
Brush was shot — hadn't Whit told her he
had shot Brush? This tucked away hideout
should prove much safer than the line camp
Ira'd suggested. Brush's friends might even-
tually have thought of that cabin.

She sank wearily down and put her back to a boulder. Brand made a long still shape in the blankets; his body at last had given up tossing and he seemed to have dropped into solid slumber. She bent toward him a moment and felt of his forehead; it didn't seem to her hand quite as hot as it had been. Perhaps, she thought with more hope than reason, he had passed the crisis and was now on the mend.

The thought comforted her.

Longer shadows were stealing across the creek bed. Tiredly she searched the sunlit rims of the canyon. No movement. How tranquil it seemed there, how out of this world. In the deep quiet the turbulence of Galeyville seemed as remote as something from another life. Her thoughts turned to Ira, and a faint disquiet that had long been with her grew to a full-blown suspicion. Why had Ira sold out his half-interest to Kane? Why hadn't he said something to them beforehand? Why had he kept it so secret — almost as though he'd been ashamed to admit he had done it? Little things, little actions of his, at the time hardly noticed but now remembered, crowded her mind with a host of dark fancies. It had been Ira, too, who had stumbled on Brand, and Ira who had insisted

Kane had no connection with her father's disappearance. It had also been Ira who'd suggested the line camp. . . .

Where was her father? Where had they taken him?

Common sense assured her he would not be harmed so long as she fell in with Kane's plans for the Luckybug. Kane must see that a threat would be more efficacious than any real harm he might do the colonel.

She didn't doubt for a minute Comstock Kane was behind the trouble.

She felt terribly drowsy. It was all she could do to keep her eyes open. Perhaps a little nap. . . . No, she dared not sleep. She must wake herself up, she must fight off exhaustion.

Far up among the rocks on the rim top, a rain crow flapped from its covert and went squawking across the canyon. The restless gurgling of the creek was a ceaseless murmur. . . .

She sat suddenly upright, fully awake. She held herself motionless, shoulders tense, listening, while her eyes flew to Brand where he lay in deep shadow beside the white-ashed remnants of the dying fire.

Then she heard it unmistakably. Horses!

She heard it again a moment later — shod hoofs striking stone.

She sprang up, badly frightened. There were two horses coming and her mind, sharp with fear, settled instantly on Brush, but a second thought told her Ben Brush would be riding at the head of a posse — he would never seek a man like Whit Brand alone. It was Ira, of course. At last he had found her; he was fetching along an extra horse for Brand. She was ashamed by remembrance of the things she had thought of him. She must not allow him to guess she'd been sleeping; he would joke about what a poor guard she was.

She tried to make out his shape through the thickening shadows. She must build up the fire, make a beacon to guide him.

She threw some fresh wood on, a handful of branches.

The leaping flames made the shadows round-about seem more intense. And then the horses came out of the shadows and stopped. The firelight shone redly on them and, with an abysmal feeling of fear, Taisy stiffened. Both horses carried riders. Neither man was McLown.

Nor was one of them Brush although, Taisy thought bitterly, one might just as well have been.

The man on the nearest horse swung down. There was a gun in his fist, and as he moved toward Whit, the look on his face pulled a scream from Taisy.

The other man laughed. "Go ahead — yell yer head off!"

The man who said that was Curly Bill.

19

PREDICTION

Of all the men who'd ever shown by their actions they intended to set the bag for Taisy, Curly Bill filled her with the most dismay. He had a dogged persistence and those things she had found to discourage other men had only filled Curly Bill with saturnine humor. "Spirit!" he'd grinned. "Thet's what I like in my string — the wilder the colt the better the hoss."

Her most calculated snubs and biting sarcasm had only increased his capacity for laughter. "Go ahead," he had told her, "fool around with these boys. Good experience for you — make you see what yer gittin' in a feller like me. I won't even bother tryin' t' scare 'em away. Hell's bells! You won't hook up with no drifter. You'll want a feller that kin pervide fer you, honey — me!" he'd said with his gusty laughter.

Bill knew his attractions. He might be

overlord of all the rustlers, but somewhere, sometime in his past, he had obviously traveled in better company and the reflection of that had not quite worn off him. He was a man who had plainly come down in the world but not, you felt sure, through any lack of talent. Some quirk in his makeup had made Bill Graham a border bandit; he might as easily have been a Butterfield, a John R. Hughes or a Mossman. His scuffed boots traveled the road to hell because he preferred to have them do so. Any old timer would be quick to tell you the best horse always makes the worst outlaw.

He was a picturesque devil with his big handsome figure. Many smart folks had fallen for his hearty laugh. There wasn't another man in Arizona Territory that could hold a candle to Bill for personality; he could make you condone him in spite of yourself. With his big burly shoulders, curly hair and dimples, he had turned plenty of female hearts and his manner with Taisy showed he did not consider hers any exception. That was what had most scared her about him, his assumption her surrender was but a matter of time. Until she'd met Whit Brand she had almost begun to believe it herself: For she'd learned one thing from her own observation, that under his cloak of jovial buffoonery, Curly Bill all the time played strictly for keeps.

He broke through her thoughts with a sudden chuckle.

"So we're aidin' an' abettin' the jail-breakers now, eh?" He clucked his tongue and shook his head at her, grinning. "I reckon you'll be makin' me a good wife yet."

Taisy flushed; then she frowned, forgetting her fright in her growing anger.

"What have you done with my father?"

Curly Bill quit laughing. Leaning forward on his pommel, he considered her alertly. "What was that?"

"You needn't look so surprised. You know my father's gone! Where have you —"

"I ain't seen your father since you an' him went foggin' up to Kane's last evenin'." He held his place, still regarding her, very evidently thinking. He was sharp enough to notice her heart was pounding; even through the shadows she could make out that much. She could see he didn't like it. He said abruptly, brusquely: "Mebbe you better be tellin' me about it. What took you up there? What happened up at Kane's?"

She raised her head and gave him back a sharp glance. As worried and frightened as she was, she could not escape his magnetism; the man's attraction was like a flame curling round her, burning her barriers, dragging her thoughts away from the wounded Whit Brand, repelling her yet, at the same time, warming her. It was beyond explaining. You might know Bill was rotten, you might know his whole record, but the man's personality affected you in spite of this. It made you wonder if you knew the real truth about him. You found yourself discounting the wild stories you had heard. It was hard to think of Bill as being as bad as he was painted.

With a shudder Taisy roused herself and quit thinking like that. She had felt that way before when he was near her. It was a power he had. She knew it for that and would not be deceived by it.

"What'd you go to Kane's for?" Bill repeated impatiently.

She told him why they had gone to see Kane, how her father had hoped the big mine owner's influence might force Ben Brush to let the stranger go.

"And what was *your* interest?"

"I went along to keep Brush from trying to shoot him again."

"You say Brush was tryin' t' shoot him? When was this?" asked Bill, surprised.

So she explained that, too, how the stranger's intervention had probably saved her father's life. But Curly Bill dismissed that much as she herself had done. He said contemptuously, "Yore father had ort to be playin' with a string of spools!" and he looked at her scathingly, ignoring her own look. "What'd you do then?"

She told him how she'd gone back to the restaurant, how Kane and her father had driven to McConaghey's, how the colonel had waited while Kane went inside and had presently got out of the mine owner's buckboard and gone off in the dark toward Jack Dall's.

"An' how do you know all that stuff?" Bill growled.

"Uncle Ira was there. He was on Mac's porch."

"An' how do you know Ira ain't mixed up in it? That deal he had with Com Kane — Hell's bells!" He glared exasperatedly at Taisy but choked off his swearing.

When he paused for breath, Taisy said: "That deal was on the level. It was after that that Dad. . . ." In the light from the fire her face looked startled. "Anyway," she said, "Ira doesn't know where my father went."

"McLown never was fit t' play with anything but spools," Curly Bill declared,
snorting. "I'm damned ef I can figger
what's got into this camp. Way folks acts
you'd think Kane had a — Hmm," he said
softly. He stared down at her sharply. "It's
plain enough why your ol' man got out of
that —"

The man with the gun, who'd been bent
over Whit, took that moment to straighten
and say disgustedly, "Treein' the marshal
don't seem to of agreed with him. Plumb
outa his head — burnin' up with fever."

"Well, now, that's too bad — fer him,"
Bill said. "Git him onto a hoss."

"Bill," Taisy cried, "if you put that man
on a horse you'll kill him!"

Curly Bill craned his neck and took a
good long look at her. "That wouldn't be
makin' no diff'rence t' you, would it?"

She felt suddenly trapped with his eyes
on her that way. She hadn't had much experience lying, but she saw that if she told the
truth Brand would never get out of that
canyon. She couldn't think what to do. She
dared not own to a personal interest and
she doubted her ability to carry off a lie.

Her continuing silence, she understood
too late, had told Curly Bill all he wanted
to know. What he read in her face stirred

his own to anger. He glared in mingled derision and contempt. He swung about in his saddle and said to the man with the pistol, "Git him on yore hoss."

"Bill —" Taisy cried, but his expression stopped her. There was black hate blazing out of his eyes and temper was making his hands shake till he could hardly keep hold of the reins. He flung them down with a curse and got out of the saddle. He grabbed a big skinning knife out of his belt and Taisy screamed and he never even looked around. He swung over to her horse and cut it loose and blasphemously drove it off into the shadows. He came back to the fire, his eyes still blazing.

Taisy's own were like marbles. She seemed scarcely to breathe. One hand was caught to the neck of her shirt and her cheeks, by the flames, looked white as a wagon sheet.

"So that's the way the wind's blowin', is it!"

He stopped, his burly shape towering over her. When she thrust out a shaking hand Bill snarled, "I ort t' blow yore brains out!" His glowering cheeks were twisted with fury and his hands were curled as though he hungered to feel them around her throat.

With a snarl he wheeled suddenly away from her. He went clanking his spurs toward his ground-hitched horse and Taisy, recalling the gun in the buggy, made a desperate try to get hold of it. But her foot skidded off a rock and she stumbled and one of her spurs hung up and pitched her. Before she could lunge to her feet Bill had her.

He hauled her up without care or politeness. He dragged her back to the firelight and struck her roughly across the face. "Tryin' fer a gun, eh?" He gave her a shove that almost flung her headlong. "Git up in that saddle!"

Taisy threw up her head, her eyes full of fire.

Curly Bill reached out and struck her again. "When I tell you t' do somethin', you jump! You ain't dealin' with no Johnny-Come-Lately. Now git up in that saddle 'fore I slap yer face off!"

The veins stood out on his neck like ropes.

Shaking and dazed, out of breath and half sick, Taisy pulled herself into it. Bill watched her, glowering. Crowder got Whit up onto the other horse and was hauling himself up behind when Bill said, "You better dust out yore think-box before you try any more tricks. You pull anythin' else an' I'll work that fine friend of yor'n over with a six-gun — savvy?"

Though an all-gone feeling was tying knots in her will power, Taisy knew enough about men to keep the fright off her face. She stared ahead of her stonily, afraid even to speak.

Bill regarded her blackly. "I ain't such a fool as a lot of folks figgers. I kin see what Kane's up to — kin see what yo're up to, too."

Her continued silence, her stony look, goaded Bill, and he swung a step nearer, one hand lifting wickedly.

"Sometimes you act like you ain't got good sense — rushin' up there t' Kane," he said scathingly. "Any kid in his diapers'd know better'n that! Kane knowed about Brand before you ever went near him. While you an' yer ol' man was traipsin' in the front, that high an' mighty Kane was lettin' Corrado out the back!"

He watched her with a vindictive grin.

She said, "I don't believe —"

"There's a passle of things you don't believe."

"But for Kane and Brush to be working together —"

"What's it look like to you? Do you think

I'd bother runnin' off with yer ol' man? I ain't interested in mines — I grab what comes outa them. You better wake up, girl — an' git this straight! That Brand won't help you. He won't git you outa this — he can't save your ol' man. Mebbe nobody can, but I'll have me a try. On one condition."

Taisy almost stopped breathing.

Curly Bill said grimly, "When we git where we're goin' I'm goin' after a preacher. If you want this guy t' keep breathin', if you want to see your ol' man agin, you'll welcome that preacher with open arms."

20

EXHIBITION OF TALENT

Dusk had come again. In the cabin it was almost dark.

Shackled by his wounds to that foul-smelling bunk with its unwashed blankets, though unspeaking and motionless Whit had not for some time been asleep or unconscious. He felt like every joint had been stretched and that broken rib never let him forget it, but the worst of his torture came from the hand Brush had driven that slug through.

But he could stand his pain; he knew pain well through first-hand acquaintance. It was the feelings of a strong man suddenly rendered helpless that made him long to yell and curse. Anger seethed through his arteries like a yeasty brew as he sought to devise some plan that would enable him to turn the tables on the men Curly Bill had left there to watch them.

Physically he was not so badly off as his

appearance indicated; he had that advantage for whatever it was worth. His fever had broken. He could think coherently. As nearly as he could figure, Bill had left two men there, Crowder and a fellow called Sandy King; King had been at the place when their party arrived. If he were to get the girl and himself clear, the effort must be made before Bill's return.

Satisfied he was alone, Whit finally opened his eyes. Dusk hemmed this room with deep shadows, but you could tell the place was a miner's shack, long abandoned by the look of it. A rusted pick and shovel, a heavy sledge and crowbar, were stacked in the corner nearest Whit's bunk. He had taken several earlier looks through his eyelids and the handle of that pick had played a part in his thinking. He wished he knew how long Bill had been gone, but he didn't.

He could, in a confused and fragmentary way, recall vague impressions of the nightmare ride that had fetched them there. He didn't know where the place was but he remembered their arrival, the surprised oaths of Sandy King. He remembered how he'd fallen trying to get off Crowder's horse, the comforting feel of Taisy's blessed arms around him — how she'd helped him inside with Bill blackly watching. But that was all. His knowledge of Bill's ultimatum, his saturnine prediction, Whit had gleaned from talk between King and Crowder. He had no notion how long he had been there.

He understood well enough why Curly Bill had fetched him. Bill would keep him alive as long as he was useful, like he was right now to strengthen Bill's hand with Taisy. Bill was still probably hoping he could make Whit divulge where the payroll money taken from the stage was cached, and Whit rather inclined toward the notion Bill was right. Whit was pretty sure he knew now where the money had got to. It had probably found its way into Comstock Kane's safe. He had overheard considerable while lying pain-racked in that bunk. King and Crowder had talked freely; there'd been no reason they shouldn't. Having pieced these scraps together, Whit had decided Brush and Kane were plainly in this thing together. As partners, on the surface, but each probably figuring to best the other. Mell Snyder was probably the key to that click robbery.

McLown had been robbed by Stampede Smith. Smith had been murdered in the Santa Ritas, probably by Brush or Corrado bent on acquiring the loot from Smith's venture. Whit thought Kane had put Smith up to it and then, when Smith had decamped with the profits, sent Brush to recover his money. Whit's reconstruction wasn't all guesswork; Smith's letters had colored Whit's thinking. It was these letters and Ira's wallet that had made Brush determined to kill him.

Kane was after the Wainright mine. Why was another story, but Whit couldn't escape that conclusion. With Ira's half-interest, which Kane had bought, and Wainright now dead or at least held prisoner, Kane probably figured to intimidate Taisy and do just about as he pleased with the mine. There wasn't any arguing Taisy's spunk, but what good was spunk against a man like Kane who held all the aces?

Whit clenched his jaws and slid both legs over the side of the bunk. This Kane was a mighty cool article. You *had* to be cool to outslick a man like Curly Bill who had made plumb fools of the U.S. Cavalry! And Kane had done it, all right. He had bought off Bill's marshal right under Bill's nose! And was getting away with it, too!

Whit didn't feel so good sitting up. The floor swayed alarmingly and his mind shied away from the thought of trying to cross it. Only the imminent likelihood of

Bill's swift return kept him from dropping down onto his back again. He had to get up. He had to cross that floor. Any play he might make to get them out of this certainly had to be made before Bill got back.

Lord, but he felt weak! Like a kitten. And the way that room kept spinning round was enough to make anyone crawl on the wagon. Maybe when he got up the damn thing would quit whirling. He thrust out his right hand and forgot and put his weight on it. He caught the hand to his chest and came off the bed doubled over, with the shock of that instant nearly setting him crazy. It was a long while before his face smoothed out and he was able to straighten his back and look round him. His eyes were still wild with pain and rage when he saw the girl, white-cheeked, in the doorway.

He pulled himself together. "I'm all right," he growled, seeing her dark, scared eyes. "Quit lookin' at me — we got t' get out of here. Where-at's them fellers Curly Bill left to watch us?"

"But your wounds!" Taisy whispered. "You hadn't ought to be up, Whit. The fever —"

"I'm all right," Whit muttered. He limped over to the corner where the tools were stacked, up-ended the pick and got the handle out of it. "They may kill me," he said, "but they'll know they been through somethin'."

"But —"

She fell silent, seeing the hard bleak look on his face. The set of his jaw told her words were useless, so when he came limping over to stand beside her, she said, "They're down below somewhere, watering the horses — at least one of them is. Crowder, I think; I don't know where King is. I haven't seen him since noon."

Hiding out, Whit thought, *with a rifle some place.*

"Where is Crowder?"

He followed her to the door, and watched when she pointed. He could see the quick rise and fall of her breathing. He stood close enough to have touched her. He looked down at the dark shapes of trees below them.

"There's a creek comes into the canyon down there, just beyond the line of those trees," Taisy said, and then: "Whit — don't chance it! Those men are armed — Whit!"

He felt her hands on him and shook them off. He went past her, not speaking. Afterwards, outside, he looked back at her briefly. It wrung her heart to see how gaunt he looked, to think of him, crippled and battered as he was, going out with a club to fight a man with a pistol.

"No matter what you hear — no matter what happens, don't leave the cabin," Whit said. "I've got to know where to find you." And he stood there another long moment as though he would engrave her face on his memory.

She was filled with a nameless fear and rushed to him. She put her hands to his shoulders and looked into his face. Her fingers touched his cheeks lightly, incredulously almost, and she grabbed him again and clung to him, trembling. "Whit!" she cried. "Whit —"

She clung to him, swaying; her sobbing lips sought his. He made a sound of despair and tore away from her roughly and wheeled, softly cursing, and started for the trees.

He knew he must be making a considerable racket but there was no way to help it. He could only hope the rushing sound of the creek would keep it from the ears of the man with the horses. The slope pitched sharply; the going was treacherous. He had to keep digging his bootheels into the shale to keep from losing what balance he had. He had to keep going to keep from thinking of Taisy.

He thought of the alley trap Brush had baited. It had come within an inch of being successful. Even now it seemed in the nature of a miracle that he had even managed to get out of there alive. Providence had certainly looked out for him. A man might almost think Brush had not really wanted actually to stop him. For a couple of heartbeats Whit toyed with that thought but was forced to discard it. Brush had aimed to, all right; he had done his best to. The marshal couldn't afford to let a man who had read Smith's letters live. True, they did not actually incriminate Brush, but Brush had hitched his wagon to Kane's bright star and what happened to Kane would encompass Kane's helpers. If Kane were ruined Brush would have to run for it, and where could Brush run to get away from Bill? Curly Bill would not forget Brush's treachery. Nor would Brush be forgetting the trouble Whit Brand had caused him. All bets were off now. Brush would get Whit Brand how and when he could. Comstock Kane himself would make sure of that.

Whit's thoughts curled again around that payroll money for the Planchas mine that had been on the stage Mell Snyder had stuck up. Snyder was Bill's man and had

231

probably been working for him. Snyder had been killed *after* the stick-up, according to Brush, who claimed to have his facts first-hand from the driver. Whit had found Snyder's body and had packed it in, thus connecting himself in Bill's mind with Mell's death. It was only logical Bill should think Whit had grabbed that money. Another thing — Bill might now believe, as it looked like Kane did, that the Wainright mine, so long considered worthless, was in actual fact a potential source of wealth. Kane's own actions would have sold Bill this notion. Bill was riding high now and meant to make the most of it. He would fetch in the preacher, bend the girl to his will, and if the mine were any good, he would have that also. And with Whit still his prisoner, he probably figured he'd still get hold of that payroll money.

Whit scanned the dark-piled shadows. He had reached the bottom of the talus slope and that line of trees was but a breath away, with their tops wind-tossed and noisy. He did not plunge into them right away. He crouched there a moment with his head cocked, listening, thinking he'd heard some cry from behind him. All he heard now was the slap of the wind. The slag-colored sky was gray with clouds and the gravelly ground beneath his feet was awhirl and crackling with autumn leaves ripped off the trees by the bitter gale.

He twisted his head and peered back toward the shack but he could not see it. He faced front again, knowing he had to go on. It had probably been some trick of the wind, but even if something were happening back there it would be too late by the time he got there. He felt like the weight of the world was on him. A kind of blackness filled his mind. He crouched in the shadows at the edge of the trees with the pick handle gripped in his good left hand and considered this dismal end he had come to. In the morning of life hope made a good breakfast but when a man came to supper he looked for something more substantial. A sense of dreary futility flowed into Whit, and he went into the grotesque piled up shadows expecting nothing better than a bullet.

His hand was stiff round the handle of the pick. Two years of marshaling Helvetia had taught him caution and he moved forward watchfully, step by step, feeling his way through the down-swinging branches. Six paces later, in their outer fringe, he froze. Statue-still he stood, with his narrowed eyes on the darker blotches of three solid shadows limned against the pale gleam of the dusk-shrouded stream.

A man and two horses.

The man was crouched at its edge, on his bootheels. He struck a match on his pants and his upswinging hand brought it cupped toward his lips from which a cigarette dangled. The horses' front feet were in the water and their down-thrust muzzles were in it also. In that second of time, while the man held his match up, the nearest horse cocked his ears and quit drinking. He lifted his head and, looking toward Whit, softly blew through his nostrils.

The man's eyes went wide in the flare of the match. His hand tensed and dropped it, and in the sudden blackness, Whit could hear him twisting around on his bootheels. He knew the man's hand would be going for his gun.

He braced himself for the bullet's impact but the man couldn't seem to make up his mind.

After all, Whit was crouched in the gloom of the branches. Perhaps the man couldn't see him and this, coupled with the recent flare of that suddenly dropped match, confused him, tending to make his judgment less critical.

But he did not at once turn away, even then. Whit could feel him staring and he held his breath. A startled curse suddenly broke from the man. He came upright.

Whit, braced and ready, with one frantic dive sprang forward and struck.

The man let go of his breath and crumpled. The near horse flung up its head and reared. Its mate lashed out wickedly with shod hind feet.

Whit had looked for this. His long knowledge of horses had warned him they'd panic and, spurred by his desperate need, he flung himself at them, wildly snatching for the reins.

His left hand missed by a good six inches, but the scared gyrations of the terrified brutes snapped the flying leathers flat across his face and he caught at them fiercely with his bandage-wrapped right. A flick of the wrist snared them firmly round it and, fighting blind pain, he hung on grimly as the lunging horses jerked and squealed. He knew they would drag him but he didn't let go.

When they finally stopped he was still on the reins. He staggered to his feet and hauled their heads down. Soothing their fears with soft curses, he quieted them. With the reins transferred to his other hand, he went over and got Crowder's gun from its holster. With grim satisfaction he shoved it into his own.

The man was still out. Whit dared not waste precious seconds tying him — indeed, he doubted if he could have managed it anyway and still have kept hold of the nervous horses. They were stout and spirited, grain fed, by their actions. They probably had good blood behind them which should make for courage and which might mean bottom. That was one thing you had to hand Curly Bill. He kept his ruffians well mounted. The best was none too good for them, and price had never stood in Bill's way.

Whit led them through the wind-whipped trees and started them up the gusty slope. It was darker now, night had fully fallen, and the dead leaves scurried and swirled underfoot. The horses pranced and blew through their nostrils, tossing their heads at each alarm. It took all Whit's depleted energy to get them started up that shaley slope.

What if Taisy weren't there? Suppose that *had* been a cry he had heard coming down there? What if King were with her — or perhaps Curly Bill, come back with his preacher!

Suddenly nervous himself, Whit tried to hurry the horses. The animals didn't want to climb that slope. They kept trying to hold back. They grew willful and stubborn, shaking their heads and sidling off sideways.

It was then, as Whit tried to think how he might mount one, that flame bit luridly out of the blackness and a gun's report hushed the night wind's crying.

21

NIGHT AND DEATH

One of the horses screamed; it was as horrible to hear as the cry of a woman. The sound of it thrashing about in the shale pinched Whit's lips together tightly, fiercely. He felt a murderous anger as he dropped its reins, bitterly fighting to hold the other horse as it tried every trick it knew to bolt past him. Taisy's voice rushed through that welter of sound, climbing high on a note of hysteria.

"Keep back!" Whit yelled; and the gun spoke again, the whine of its bullet laying a thin track of sound as it tunneled the nearby blackness.

Whit knew he had to get out of there. He couldn't fire back with his gun hand swathed like it was in bandages; he couldn't use the other hand and still hold the horse.

He knew the man was firing by sound; it was too much to think he could see through that blackness. The man was laying his fire by the sounds from Whit's horse and, though he saw it was only a question of time till the law of averages took care of his account, Whit never once thought of casting the animal loose. He would sooner be shot than left afoot.

It wasn't anger so much that drove him now. He was gripped by a sense of tremendous urgency. He kept crowding the horse, trying to turn him uphill, throwing all the weight he could fetch on the reins in an effort to drag down his raised head. The horse fought every inch of the way, and to make matters worse, through and around all the rest of the racket, Whit could hear the rushed pounding of oncoming boots and he bitterly cursed the girl's bullheadedness.

Then he suddenly realized it wasn't Taisy who was charging across that shale toward him. He could hear her dim cry from a different direction and despair rushed over him, hammering the last bit of hope from his mind. This was King rushing in to make sure of his target.

Desperately Whit took both feet off the ground. The horse's head came down and its hind feet lashed out. He tried to shake Whit loose. In a frenzy of fear he commenced savagely bucking. Whit groaned at the slivers of pain that came down his arm from that bullet-torn hand, but he anchored it round the cheek strap, sobbing, and twisted his left, with the reins, in its mane. He struck out with his feet and kicked himself upward. The horse's sudden lunge flung him onto its back, and clinging there, shaking, he let the animal bolt.

Straight for the trees it went like an arrow.

It took every ounce of strength Whit had to turn the horse before they struck the trees, but Whit did it. The horse whirled round in a careening half-circle and Whit drove it straight for the slope again. They went up through the shale like a rocket and Whit could see sparks fly from each strike of its hoofs. Flame knifed out of the blackness before him. He drove the horse at it wickedly. A man's scream was shrill with fright as they struck and went over him.

Whit got the horse stopped.

Taisy's voice came out of the darkness anxiously.

Whit looked toward the sound with haunted eyes.

"Whit!" Taisy cried.

"Here," he said, and walked the trembling horse toward her voice. Whit was like a wrung out rag in that moment. He had hardly enough strength to stay upright. He was afraid he would fall before the horse reached her, but they made it.

"Are you all right, Whit?"

It was good to know someone cared for him. Perhaps her care was born only of need; reason told him this was so, but it warmed him anyway to know she cared even that much. He had never had anyone to care for him before.

"Take the reins," he said, letting them slide from his hand; and the next thing he knew she was trying to lift him off the ground.

"Try, Whit — please! You've got to let me get some food inside you. Please! You *can't* quit now!"

He made an effort to get up; he didn't know if he succeeded. He kept dropping off, drifting in and out of short stretches of consciousness. But she was always there with him, always fussing over him, always doing something for him or trying to get him to do something for her. He remembered eating; it wasn't the sort of food he customarily took. Once he thought he felt her lips on his forehead, but in his fully awake moments that seemed unlikely.

He was more awake now. She was holding another cup of coffee to his mouth. The heat of it, the fragrant taste, felt good to his parched throat. Then he remembered the man he'd left down on the creek bank.

She pushed him back.

He said, "That Crowder —"

"I've tied him. Drink your coffee. I've got the horse all saddled."

"Have you got any idea whereabouts we are?"

"We're in Pantano Canyon, if I've got my directions fixed right."

"About how far would that be from your father's mine?" Whit asked, and he saw her eyes grow startled.

She drew away a little. Her staring eyes kept watching him. She moved away a little farther and got swiftly to her feet.

He didn't understand her look.

"Why would you be asking?"

He didn't get her look at all. And then he thought he did, and sighed.

He waited another dragging moment and then irritably said, "What's the matter now? You ain't thinkin' *I* grabbed him, are you?"

She took her time about answering. Her eyes kept staring tightly with that pinched and bitter look. He felt his dander rising as silence settled thickly.

Taisy's eyes began to blaze. The shakiness of anger was in the voice with which she said, "So that is where you've put him!" and a flood of words poured out of her. "So I was right! You're just a gunslick — just a cheap gun-throwing drifter! What a fool I've been!" Her laugh was harsh, an ugly sound that bordered on hysteria. She started backing toward the door.

He could almost see her thoughts taking shape. She meant to grab that horse and leave him.

As Whit flung himself to his feet she whirled. Her hand caught the door and pulled it open.

Curly Bill, gun in hand, stood framed there, grinning.

22

THE WATERHOLE

They were caught, all right. They were
caught flat-footed. Whit didn't need to see
Crowder back of Bill's shoulder to know
they were finally, irrevocably stopped. With
the girl's slim shape in front of Bill that way,
Whit had no choice. He raised his hands up
level with his shoulders and bitterly heard
Bill's gusty laugh.

Bill said, still grinning, "You're lookin'
rather flushed, my dear. You weren't
thinkin' of quittin' my tender care?" He
laughed again in his boisterous way to see
the way frustration shook her.

"Never mind," he said. "If it's a trip you
crave you shall hev yore way. I didn't git
time to contact no preacher, I come damn
near runnin' into Earp an' his crowd. I was
kinda worried, too, thinkin' mebbe you
might up an' git out of here some way.
'Course I knowed you wouldn't do it on
yore own free will. But I says to myself, I

says, 'Curly, you dang ol' hossthief, you better git you back to yore true lovin' woman.' "

He broke off to slap his thigh and guffaw. His black eyes gleamed, his white teeth flashed. "Yep," he declared, "that's jest what I told myself. 'You better git you back to yore true lovin' Taisy afore that egg-suckin' gun-fighter up and runs off with her.' An' how right I was!" he said, eyeing Brand sneeringly.

Whit said nothing. There was nothing to say.

Bill cuffed at his chaps and considered Brand narrowly. "Figured t' run off with my sweet little bullfinch." He scowled, and said grimly: "Mebbe you figured t' help me round up that preacher."

His face turned ugly. He breathed at Whit softly, "You'll git yore wish, bucko. You'll see a preacher — there's one I know t'other side of the Whetstones. We're goin' over there now, all four of us. An' while we're ridin' you better be recallin' whereabouts it was you cached that mazuma."

One moment longer Curly Bill looked at Whit; then he slammed his bull voice like a hammer at Crowder. "Fetch up my hoss."

Crowder turned at once and faded into the darkness.

At Coyote Smith's, near dawn, Bill stopped to pick up fresh horses, including a couple for Whit and the girl. All through the black shank of night they had ridden, till Whit felt stiff as the proverbial board. He'd had time for considerable thinking and had several times wondered if Bill's mention of a preacher might not be a red herring designed to cover up the real purpose of this ride. There had been little talking. All Bill's energies seemed directed toward speed, speed and then more speed. You would almost have thought Bill was running from something.

At Smith's Bill picked up a couple more men: a pair of whiskered ruffians that were armed to the teeth.

Smith served them a steaming breakfast which the outlaws ate in a wolfish silence broken only by the clatter of their dishes. Bill didn't even give them time for a smoke. He swabbed out his plate with the back of a biscuit. "You kin smoke while we're ridin'. Come along an' git at it."

They rode steadily till noon, stopping only for horses. Mile after weary mile they rode, through a sandy waste grown to catclaw and greasewood. The long valley shimmered with the heat, and there were times when Whit looked ready to fall from the saddle, so whipped out was he by constant riding.

Finally temper got the best of him. "What's the rush?" he cried, exasperated. "You got the U.S. Cavalry camped on your back trail?"

Curly Bill sent a snarl back over his shoulder. "You better save yer wind t' dig up that loot with!"

It was late afternoon when they rode into a narrow depression between the Whetstone Mountains and the Mustangs. "Iron Springs up ahead," Bill said, waving a hand. "We'll hole up there till moonrise."

Whit saw a grove of small trees up ahead around a pool. It made a lush blotch of green against the glare of the blistering sands. The tall cottonwoods threw down a welcome shade and through gaps in the willows you could see the sun glinting off the white water. It was a lovely sight, cool and shady and peaceful, and Taisy loosed a glad cry when she saw it.

They rode into the trees and unsaddled their horses, upending their saddles and spreading their sweat-soaked saddle blankets on them. The outlaws hobbled their horses and let them fan out to browse. Then they followed Bill over to the south of the pool where there was a kind of embankment and there, in the shade, they stretched themselves out while Crowder got a fire going and, with the sack of food Bill had fetched from Smith's, prepared to throw together some sort of a meal.

They were tired and hot and Whit, for one, was hungry. Curly Bill flopped down on the end of a log and commenced rolling up a brown-paper smoke.

"By Gawd," he said, letting a good strong puff of it seep through his nostrils, "it's about time we was gittin' out of this country. We been crowdin' our luck about as far as we kin. There ain't many left of the ol' bunch; we been losin' men fast in the last couple months. I'm as tough as the next, but I'm a-gittin' right tired of the screech of blue whistlers. One of these days I'm liable t' git on my hoss an' just keep right on ridin'."

"Where you figurin' t' go?" one of the whiskered gents asked. "You goin' t' take us with you?"

"Them as wants to kin come. I got a hankerin' t' see what she's like in Chihuahua." He sent a grin at Taisy. "How'd you like t' see Chihuahua, baby?"

"You're headin' wrong fer Chihuahua," Crowder said. "We're ridin' plumb away from it."

"Oh, I ain't goin' yet. Got a couple little chores t' git done up round here first. Cripes, we kin live like kings down there; we got plenty put by, even after we split it. A man's a fool not t' quit when he's got him enough."

Whit wasn't interested in Bill's philosophy. He was thinking again of Stampede Smith, the man from whose pockets he had got McLown's wallet and Taisy's picture. But it was not of those things he was thinking just then. He was remembering those letters Mr. Smith had had on him. They'd been signed with the name of Comstock Kane. The first had proposed a meeting with Smith at what Whit judged to have been some out of the way place where they wouldn't be likely to be seen together. The second letter looked, the way it was wrinkled, like it had been wrapped around something. Banknotes, probably. The sheet contained but one sentence of writing, and no signature. *Part cost*, it said, *of freighting in one melodian*. Whit doubted that strongly. It was much more likely to have been the down payment on something too shady to be trusted to writing. Smith's possession of the wallet probably told the story.

Smith had tried to beat Kane and had been rubbed out. Whit could understand that, but why had Kane suddenly closed down the Planchas? Not for a moment did Whit believe the reason given. Kane wasn't the sort to be stopped by stage robbers — particularly by robbers he himself was hiring. And he must have been hiring them. Whit had given this angle considerable thought and was pretty well satisfied that most of that money was going back to Kane — how else was the man able to meet his payrolls? The burning question, to Whit's mind, was why Kane would be closing down a property the operation of which wasn't costing him a cent.

There was a *reason* Kane might find it profitable to close down a paying job like the Planchas; there was a mighty good reason and Whit was pretty certain he could put the name to it. Kane wasn't out of ore, but he might well have discovered his precious Planchas was apexed, that the ore he was mining belonged by rights to the colonel.

All Kane's men, though the bulk of their time was spent lapping up booze in the Galeyville bars, were still on the payroll.

He was holding those men against a plan to reopen. He was after control of the Luckybug Lode and Whit was willing to bet that, once he got it, Kane would promptly close it and reopen the Planchas. It might start tongues wagging if the Planchas stayed closed and Kane began mining Planchas-type ore from the Wainright tunnel. A smart operator like Kane wouldn't risk it. He would rather be laughed at for an act of philanthropy, for having thrown away the money to save Wainright's face.

Whit nodded, frowning. Yes, the irony of that would appeal to Kane hugely. Then another thought struck him, almost proving the truth of his conjectures. Of course the careful Kane would be keeping his men on; some of them might know, or guess, as much as himself! He'd be playing it close until he knew which ones. This was a country where knowledge could be hard on the health. Smith hadn't been killed because he'd double-crossed Kane. Smith had been silenced to make sure he *stayed* silent. That same kind of fate might overtake the colonel.

On the other hand, Kane might try to play this cute. He didn't have to have the colonel's signature at all; he could grab

Wainright's mine on a forged set of papers or he could manage it through the girl — always providing, of course, he kept old Jim out of sight. This would be, in the event he ever got tripped up, less dire in its penalty than deliberate murder; it would leave him quite a choice of passably plausible explanations, whereas murder offered nothing but a hangman's rope. And if he *could* get the colonel to sign the Luckybug over. . . .

The problem was to figure where the devil Kane would hold him. Where, Whit asked himself, could Wainright be held against his will without involving Kane, or anyone, in the event Jim was discovered?

The answer, when it came to Whit, shoved cold chills through his belly.

One of the outlaws got up to stare out over the valley. He stretched himself and scratched his chest. He turned his head and said to Bill, "What the hell would you do, Curly, if you was t' meet Wyatt Earp right now?"

"By Gawd," Bill growled, "I'd kill him."

"You better git yore gun cocked then. Five fellers an' Earp is out there now. They're headin' right fer this water hole!"

"Wyatt Earp?" Bill's gusty laugh boomed. "I wisht the hell he *was!*" he said. He pitched the butt of his smoke away and got to his feet and froze there, staring. With a curse he jumped for his rifle and the rest of the outlaws grabbed for theirs.

Whit rolled over and came upright, frantic. He took one look and ran toward Taisy. There were horsemen out there all right, at least six of them. "Git down!" he yelled. "Git down — git down!"

Taisy stared at him blankly. She opened her mouth. Whit knocked her, sprawling, into the brush and flung himself down beside her.

Crowder, by the fire, came out of his crouch. He dropped his pan and whirled to run. Curly Bill caught his shoulder, flung him back. "You're in this, too! What's the matter with you? That bank'll protect you — I been waitin' months fer a break like this. Git over there, damn you!"

He slanched a look at the others, waiting till Crowder took a place in the line. "Now! Give it to 'em!" he yelled, and the whole crew rose up and emptied their rifles.

Surprise, terror, confusion gripped the milling riders out there in the open. Horses reared, squealing. Two went down. One flung up its heels and bucked round in a circle, increasing the din, the crazy shouting. One man went off the rump of his horse with his mouth stretched wide in an unheard yell. Whit saw Wyatt Earp unsling his shotgun and get down off his horse, coolly slipping his left arm through the bridle reins. He watched the ex-marshal of Tombstone bring the shotgun's butt carefully up to his shoulder. He was sighting the weapon at Curly Bill where half of Bill's body showed above the bank. Bill was crouched a little forward, squinting at Earp down the barrel of his rifle. Whit could see the pressure of the outlaw's finger tighten, and that was when Earp pulled both triggers.

Curly Bill staggered back with the strangest expression. The rifle clattered from his hand. He gave a terrible yell. His knees suddenly folded and he pitched forward on his face with that demoniacal yell fading into a gurgle.

Crowder whirled, cursing, and broke for the horses. Dust jumped out of the back of his vest and he threw up both arms and went down like a steer at the end of a rope.

Hardly three seconds had passed, Whit judged, from the time Bill had rapped out that order to fire. Yet no one was outside the cottonwoods now but Earp and the man who'd been gunned from his horse.

The Lion of Tombstone had dropped his shotgun and was reaching across the saddle for his rifle. The rest of his crowd were fanning the dust in a mad race for safety. By the unflurried calm of the man's cool actions, you would never have guessed Earp stood there alone. You'd have thought his whole clan was right behind him, and maybe he did.

From where Whit lay, thirty feet away, he could see two holes through the crown of Earp's hat, and how the sides of the brim, cut loose by bullets, hung down and flapped foolishly about his ears. He could see ragged rents in the seams of Earp's pants and how the bottom of his coat, where his gun sheaths held it out from his body, was slashed by lead until it looked like a flutter of ribbons tied there. Yet there the man stood trying to get at his rifle.

"Earp's horse," Whit afterwards said, "was scared stiff." It began to rear and squeal and plunge and Earp couldn't get the rifle out of its scabbard. He yanked out one of his pistols then and, ducking around behind the half crazed bronc, opened fire on the outlaws from under its neck. He threw one shot across the top of the saddle.

Bill's men didn't care for that kind of fighting. They must have known Bill was down, for he had quit his yelling, and neither one of them had bargained to find himself swapping shots with the man who had run them out of Tombstone. The biggest whiskered gent dropped below the bank and scuttled like a crab toward Bill's sprawled shape, and the other whiskered ruffian, suddenly discovering himself alone, let out a scared bleat and headed for the horses.

It must have been about then that Wyatt Earp looked around, probably to see how his companions were making out. Whit had no means of knowing what Earp's survey disclosed, but the man must have realized Bill's bunch had quit shooting. He sent a couple more slugs across the embankment and commenced, step by step, to fade out of the picture, doing what he could to keep his horse between himself and the willow brush fringing the outlaws' covert.

This was no easy task. The terrified horse was well nigh unmanageable. Earp must have wondered why no bullets followed him, but not enough to make him want to investigate. He seemed quite satisfied to leave and let well enough alone. He kept right on backing, and when he had gone about sixty yards he threw up a leg and tried to fork his saddle. But his cartridge belt had slipped so low he couldn't get his right leg over the cantle. He had to drop back and adjust it. Then he vaulted to the saddle and fed his bronc the steel. They departed like he was trying to break a quarter-mile record.

Whit got to his feet and took a quick look around. While he'd been watching Earp, the two outlaws had flung their saddles on a couple of the horses, knocked off the hobbles and, with one of them supporting Bill's limp shape before him, were now flogging off like the devil was trying to catch hold of their shirttails.

Whit helped Taisy up and ran over to Crowder. There was nothing Whit could do for him short of a shovel. He passed up the desire to take a look at Earp's man; Earp's bunch would be back for him as soon as dark fell. The common-sense thing for Whit to do was get out of there.

He lost no time saddling the best-looking pair of the remaining four horses. Taisy evidenced no regret at leaving the place, and, having loosed the other horses, they took off at a lope heading south by east.

"You know where we're goin'?" Whit asked abruptly.

"The way we're going right now we're heading for Tombstone."

"Good enough," Whit nodded. "That'll suit me fine. We'll pick up the sheriff an' be ridin' with authority. I've had all the ridin' with crooks I'm a-wantin'."

He wished he were smart enough to say something cheering. Taisy looked like she was skating mighty close to the edge. But the thoughts in his head right then were not of a kind to cheer up anyone. It was imperative they get to Galeyville just as quickly as fast horses could fetch them. At the risk of alarming her, he stepped up the pace.

Her eyes studied him anxiously. "Are we being followed?" she asked. She looked over her shoulder.

"Can't be sure," Whit said. "I'm playin' it safe." He gave the buckskin its head and felt its stride reach out. Both horses still had a lot of miles left in them, but he had to make them last until he could get his hands on fresh ones. Twice they saw ranches and Whit changed their course to miss them. "Hard to tell in this country who's a friend and who isn't. We'll nurse what we've got an' hope they'll get us to Tombstone —"

"But, Whit," Taisy cried, "Wyatt Earp wouldn't bother us."

"He won't if he don't ketch us."

Let her think what she wanted. Let her think him afraid. Whit could not tell her he was pushing the pace out of fear for her father. Yesterday Whit had thought he had Kane figured, that the man's cautious nature would keep Wainright alive. Now he was not sure. It seemed to him now that Kane's instinct for caution might suddenly persuade him to do away with Wainright.

Look at it Kane's way. The colonel, alive, was a continuing menace. Dead, he would keep his mouth shut; and Taisy if she weren't already, would be too discouraged after her father's death to fiddle much longer with what, all too plainly, was a worthless property. Of course the mine wasn't worthless, but Kane would make it appear so. The whole thing depended on his properly engineering the colonel's death. Proper engineering would show the death as natural — as due, that is, to natural causes; and this was what now bothered Whit. He had seen how the thing could dovetail neatly to bring about the very impression Kane was after; every ingredient, every tool, was available. And

Kane was too shrewd an operator not to have made this discovery himself.

Wainright might be dead now, but if he wasn't he soon would be, if Whit had got this thing figured right. In the first place, Kane would have seen at once he could not afford to be identified with the colonel's disappearance. From snatches of talk he had heard and remembered, Whit knew the two had driven to McConaghey's and Kane had gone in, leaving the colonel to wait for him. But Wainright, apparently fed up with waiting, had left Kane's buckboard before the man returned, and in the gathering dusk had set off up the street. There was nothing in that to attach blame to Kane. How, then, had Kane worked it?

He must have had help. He must, on one pretext or another, have suggested that Wainright do exactly what he had done. By the time Wainright reached the place he'd been heading for, obviously Kane had got his plans perfected. Kane's helper, either Brush or Corrado very likely, had been waiting for Wainright and had overpowered him. Since Kane could not risk having someone caught guarding the colonel, he had plainly had to put him where he wouldn't need guarding. What more logical place could he have found for this purpose than the place where Whit now believed him to be?

Kane had, of necessity, to work his wiles with but one or two helpers. The more underlings involved the more risk he'd be courting. And he was bound to have foreseen these would have to be silenced. Brush and Corrado already shared his confidence to some extent; so he would use one of them — Corrado, most likely. The coup would not take long. Corrado could waylay Wainright and tie him up some place. Kane could then pick up Wainright, bound, gagged and blindfolded, and in a matter of minutes whisk him out to the mine — for that was where they would find Taisy's father, if they found him at all, down in one of the stopes of the Luckybug Lode.

No better hiding place for Wainright could be hit on than the man's own mine. Who would look for him there? He'd been working it himself, without help, for months. And who, if the old man was discovered, would connect his presence there with Comstock Kane? Obviously, no one.

Kane might not have employed any helper in the colonel's abduction. He might have handled the whole thing himself. Certainly he could have. A man resourceful as Kane appeared to be would have considered all the angles and have taken care of them.

Were Kane to get desperate, he could let it be known, among those of his miners he suspected of being cognizant of what was behind the Planchas shutdown, that he had reason to fear Wainright's mine had them apexed. Since this was what they already guessed, it would take no great amount of urging on Comstock Kane's part to send them into Wainright's mine to find out. A match would then take care of Kane's problems. He could bring that whole face of the mountain down and he was the kind of a man who would do it.

23

NEW BLOOD

On blowing horses Whit and Taisy crested
a ridge and saw the lights of Tombstone.
They cantered east on Bruce through the
horse-tracked dust until the dark shuttered
shape of the Episcopal church showed
against the lamp gleams from the main part
of town. They turned right, then, going
south on Third at an easy walk designed to
call no attention to themselves. Past the
photo shop and the stage barns they moved
like a couple of ghosts doing midnight duty;
then Whit suddenly stopped with a muttered oath. He raked a glance up Allen
Street, then looked at the girl. They had to
have fresh horses. It might attract unfavor-
able notice if he took the girl with him to
the O.K. Corral; on the other hand, he
dared not leave her there — he'd heard too
many tales in the last few months about the
kind of a place this Tombstone was. The
horses could wait; he'd see the sheriff first.

He picked up his reins and gave the girl a nod. "We'll go see the sheriff an' git the horses later."

They continued down Third, swung right on Tough Nut and then turned left, riding into the courthouse yard and pulling up by the hitchrack fronting the building. Whit dismounted stiffly and helped the girl down. It squeezed his heart to see how she looked. He patted her shoulder with a shy man's gruffness and made sure the pistol he had taken off Crowder was loose in his holster. Taisy sagged with weariness. She was too spent to talk and followed him numbly into the building.

There was a light in the sheriff's office and the door stood open.

A man with his chair propped against the wall was dozing, with his spurred boots braced against the desk. He opened one eye and considered them uncharitably, noting the trail dust powdering their clothing, Whit's bandaged hand and battered features.

"You the sheriff?" Whit asked.

"Under-sheriff — name's Woods."

"I'd like to see the sheriff."

"You'll prob'ly hev quite a wait. Johnny's out with a posse chasin' Wyatt Earp's outfit."

"Any chance of you ridin' out to Galey-ville with us?"

"Not a chance. I'm anchored to this office till the sheriff gits back. What's the matter out there?"

"We need a little law."

The man put his feet down and grinned at Whit sourly. "You better see Brush — he's the marshal over there."

"It happens he's mixed up in it."

"Well, that's shore too bad. Like to help you," Woods said, "but we got all we kin handle takin' care of Tombstone. Hell, we can't even collect the taxes over there."

"Couldn't you spare us a deputy?"

Woods shook his head. "Only feller we've got who'd dare go into the camp is Billy Breakenridge, an' you can't hev him because he's gone with the sheriff."

Whit dared waste no more time. "Can this young lady stay here until I round up fresh horses?"

"You bet. Hev a chair, ma'am. Would you like some hot cawffee?"

In the ghostly gloom that shrouded the false dawn the tunnel mouth was black and forbidding, but Whit was glad to see it. They had come far and fast, changing horses three times, and the girl had held

265

up her end like a veteran. She had asked no questions, though she must have wondered at Whit's driving pace, and when at last he had told her the situation as he saw it, she had gritted her teeth and kept her chin up. No tears. Whit was proud of her.

He had done a pile of thinking in the dark hours of the night and he had, he thought, solved the problem of Mell Snyder and what had become of that payroll money Mell had stopped the stage for. It was the lack of tracks that had thrown Whit off all along, and it was this same lack of tracks that had finally convinced him. He'd assumed at first that the tracks had been rubbed out, but now he knew there never had been any tracks but Snyder's. The shotgun guard had killed Snyder with a pistol. It was the only answer that would fit all the facts.

Whit stopped their horses in a thicket of cedars.

He'd been afraid that when Kane learned Whit had escaped Brush's trap, the man would put his plans in motion and set off the charges that would cave in Wainright's mine. But there was the tunnel mouth now, black and frowning.

They got out of their saddles. Vaguely showing off yonder were the tents and tarpaper shanties that housed the miners who worked in Kane's Planchas. These were dark at that hour and looked completely deserted. Beyond them loomed the Planchas hoist. Nowhere could Whit's narrowed gaze descry any movement.

Through the gray half-light he looked soberly at Taisy. "You can help me now, Taisy. I want you to stay with these horses — Listen to me! If your Dad's really in there Kane may have someone watchin'. What's your Dad goin' to do if we both git grabbed?"

"But —"

"Listen, girl — trust me! Do what I tell you; this is no time to argue. If anything happens when you see me go in there, you git in the saddle an' make for town in a hurry. Tell 'em your story — tell 'em Kane's found out you've got the Planchas apexed; the ore he's been minin' wasn't his to mine. Tell 'em he's holdin' your Dad prisoner in the Luckybug Lode — tell 'em Kane is the one that's been grabbin' them payrolls. Will you do that, Taisy?"

"Yes, but —"

"Good girl!" Whit cried, and whirled away at once, darting into the open beyond the dark branches. It twisted his heart to leave her that way, but it was best. If he had stayed in her presence any longer the things that were locked in his heart might betray him. He had no right to tell her he loved her, not while he faced the dangerous task still before him. It would be hard enough for her to lose her Dad. . . .

He struck up a stumbling run through the grayness, through the night's last gloom that still clung to the rocks and short brush round the mine front, finding himself more shaky than he'd thought but fighting against it, fighting his unexpected shortness of wind, fighting time and despair and the black futility that made his own mind laugh and jeer at his efforts to snatch a trapped man out of that doomed hole.

Only twenty yards more and still no sign of Kane's watcher. Where was the man? In the mine itself? Fiercely Whit's narrowed eyes raked the gloom as his boots took him up that talus slope, but he saw no movement, no crouched shape, no slightest sign that would tend to confirm his desperate fears. Then he understood. This was the payoff; the final act was at hand! Kane would be glad to have him in there, trapped with the rest, when the blast went off.

He ripped the bandage off his maimed

hand, wincing as he flexed cramped fingers, locking his teeth against the pain. He drew the borrowed gun from his holster, grimly fitting his hand about it, and that way climbed the face of the dump. He came against the mine's timbered entrance, and tried to hear against the pounding of his heart and the grinding wheeze of his tortured lungs. He tried to see through the blackness before him; and it was then he heard far-off voices, sepulchral, thinned to ghostly whispers by the twists and turns of unseen stopes.

He went into the tunnel's pulsating darkness, forward crouched, head canted, striving to catch those whispers of sound again, striving to learn if he had really heard them; and was like that when he caught the advance of a booted foot.

He tried to whirl, to throw himself sideways, to whip up the gun and trip its trigger, but his weakened muscles seemed weighted with lead. Blackness waved and danced around him, heaving, pitching like a fractious bronc. And the tunnel floor reared suddenly upright and dragged its claws across his face.

He was down — he knew that. It wasn't the tunnel floor rushing over him. It was himself being dragged across the tunnel floor, deeper and deeper into that blackness; he could hear the grunting breath of the dragger, the rasp of the dragger's boots against stone. He could hear, but he had no strength to fight. He lay without movement where the man's hands dropped him, listening to the hollow boom of his retreat while the blackness gibbered and jumped about him.

No — that was crazy. It was himself he heard, and he tried to make out what he was saying, but it was all mixed up with the voices that came flying up from the stopes below. They were running now. He could hear the rasp and bang of their boots, or perhaps it was his own he heard. He was on his feet, he knew that much, but his movements didn't seem to have much direction. Groping, stumbling like a tenderfoot running in circles, staggering back from one wall only to bring up crash-bang against the other.

It might help, he thought, if he put up a hand. But the one he tried to bring up was too heavy. He reckoned he was too played out to do it. But the other came up of its own volition, and when it did what he told it, he heard himself laugh and its craziness scared him.

He sucked in his breath and clamped his

jaws on the sound. He stared till he found a dim gray oblong, paying no heed to the gradually louder voices. He could focus on only one thing at a time, and right now it was important that he head for that grayness that vaguely showed through the black up ahead.

Twice he fell, and once he lay a while, shaking and retching, before memory again forced him onto his feet. It took him a while to get his legs under him and then the damned things wouldn't half mind him. He eased himself down onto his hands and knees and scrabbled on in that way, vaguely aware of the mounting racket from the swollen and tumultuous voices behind him.

He lifted his head and sleeved the sweat from his eyes. Hardly twenty feet now lay between him and the brighter gray of the tunnel mouth. It came over him suddenly why he had to reach it and he staggered erect and shambled toward it.

There were men there, two of them, two black shapes against that rectangle of brightening day. One stood over something with a match in his hand — Whit saw the leap of the tiny flame, heard a peculiar splutter that grew into a hiss as the second man leaped toward the first, bringing his lifted arm down sharply. The first man swayed, lost his balance and crumpled. Whit saw the other man whirl and run.

It was Taisy's scream that brought Whit out of his exhausted stupor. Whit couldn't see her but the running man did. He was at the entrance. He stopped to whip up an arm and fired. Flame jumped out of his lifted hand and the sound of that shot flung back through the passage like the crash of a thousand rifles.

In that moment Whit's heart turned completely still. Scarcely breathing, he stared with horrified eyes. He had never imagined Kane would try to kill Taisy.

His teeth flashed in a snarl of rage. He sprang forward like a man possessed. The sight and sound of that flaming pistol had roused him as no other thing could have. Something burst inside him. All the goodness and mercy, all the boyish tolerance that ever had tempered Whit's dealings with others, rushed out of his face and left it as barren as sun-bleached bone.

He could see Kane then with steel-etched clarity. He saw nothing else, he heard no sound. He never remembered lifting a hand — that bullet-torn hand that still gripped his pistol — nor the bright tongue of flame that belched red from its muzzle. He was conscious of nothing save the sight of Kane twisting with agonized eyes, of Kane's mouth stretched wide in a soundless yell, of his legs buckling under him, causing him to sprawl like a ripped-open sack.

It was then Whit remembered the men trapped in the mine — Kane's whole devilish purpose; and he whirled with blanched cheeks. Whirled and stopped with a wondrous sigh. It was all right now; the men were coming. There they were, just yonder, pressing noisily toward him, talking, laughing, gesticulating, swearing — and then Whit swore, too, as his eyes suddenly fell on that hissing fuse. It was short — too short! There were not two inches of unburned fuse left!

Whit flung himself at it.

A terrific pain ran through him. He felt himself lifted, and then he didn't feel anything until something cool washed over his forehead and his opened eyes looked into Taisy's anxious, starry, compassionate bright ones.

"Bravest thing I ever seen!" someone kept saying over and over, and there were peering faces all about him, and Whit realized suddenly he had his head in Taisy's lap, and got up self-consciously. Friendly hands came out to him, and Taisy stood by him holding onto his arm like she didn't mean ever to let it go. And Whit said, kind of hot around the neck of his collar, "I sure been actin' like a weanin' filly," and the miners grouped about him laughed.

"You done all right, boy," one of them grinned. "Bravest thing I ever seen the way you jumped at thet box an' grabbed out the fuse bare-handed. If there's any a favor you ever want jes' call on me, Chuck Rankin, any time." And another man clapped Whit's shoulder, and the colonel was there, and Brush, with a couple of big miners hanging onto his arms.

A little man surged up to Whit and said, "You sure done plenty. But one thing I'd like to ask you — how'd you git wise Kane was grabbin' them payrolls?"

"It had to be Kane," Whit said, and told them how he'd found Snyder's body with no tracks around it but Snyder's own. "The guard or the driver killed Snyder with a belt gun. If they ain't skipped out you can likely twist it out of them. They shot Mell Snyder an' drove right off. The express box they probably heaved over the cliffs. Then they come into town an' reported the robbery. Also, they handed over to Kane them two sacks of ore the assayer at Tucson sent back to him — they handed Kane the sacks, but I don't think them sacks held ore any more. It's my guess them sacks held Kane's payroll money. I think he had it insured an' was collectin' both ways."

Several miners nodded. One or two made unpleasant remarks about Kane's ancestry. Then the colonel stepped up beside Whit and Taisy. He put a hand on Whit's arm, the arm whose hand was again wrapped in bandages. The colonel said, "Words ain't much use at a time like this, son. You've done more for me than I kin ever repay."

"Shucks," Whit said, and Taisy's eyes smiled brightly, which was a heap more pay than any saddle bow slim of a drifter had coming.

"We're doin' considerable hopin' you'll want to locate here," the colonel told him fervently. "The Luckybug needs new blood to work it and. . . ." He let his voice trail off, suddenly chuckling as his eyes caught the look between Whit and his daughter.

"I guess, boys," he said with a wink at the others, "we'll be a heap more useful somewheres else." A pair of them clapped each other's backs, they all trouped off and Colonel Wainright followed, looking mighty like the cat with the goldfish inside him.

Whit looked worriedly at Taisy.

"Do you reckon you could care for a cheap driftin' gunslick?"

"I sure could, if you'd take to a girl with freckles."

About the Author

Nelson Nye was born in Chicago, Illinois. He was educated in schools in Ohio and Massachusetts and attended the Cincinnati Art Academy. His early journalism experience was writing publicity releases and book reviews for the *Cincinnati Times-Star* and the *Buffalo Evening News*. In 1935 he began working as a ranch hand in Texas and California and became an expert on breeding quarter horses on his own ranch outside Tucson, Arizona. Much of this love for horses can be found in exceptional novels such as *Wild Horse Shorty* and *Blood of Kings*. He published his first Western short story in *Thrilling Western* and his first Western novel in 1936. He continued from then on to write prolifically, both under his own name and the by-lines Drake C. Denver and Clem Colt. During the Second World War, he served with the U.S. Army Field Artillery. In

1949–1952 he worked as horse editor for *Texas Livestock Journal*. He was one of the founding members of the Western Writers of America in 1953 and served twice as its president. His first Golden Spur Award from the Western Writers of America came to him for best Western reviewer and critic in 1954. In 1958–1962 he was frontier fiction reviewer for the *New York Times Book Review*. His second Golden Spur came for his novel *Long Run*. His virtues as an author of Western fiction include a tremendous sense of authenticity, an ability to keep the pace of a story from ever lagging, and a fecund inventiveness for plot twists and situations. Some of his finest novels have had off-trail protagonists such as *The Barber of Tubac*, and both *Not Grass Alone* and *Strawberry Roan* are notable for their outstanding female characters. His books have sold over 50,000,000 copies worldwide and have been translated into the principal European languages. The *Los Angeles Times* once praised him for his "marvelous lingo, salty humor, and real characters." Above all, a Nye Western possesses a vital energy that is both propulsive and persuasive.